COMMUNITY
KLEPTO

COMMUNITY KLEPTO

a novel

KELLY I. HITCHCOCK

SHE WRITES PRESS

Published 2022
Printed in the United States of America

Print ISBN: 978-1-64742-373-5
E-ISBN: 978-1-64742-374-2
Library of Congress Control Number: 2021925636

For information, address:
She Writes Press
1569 Solano Ave #546
Berkeley, CA 94707

She Writes Press is a division of SparkPoint Studio, LLC. All company and/or product names may be trade names, logos, trademarks, and/or registered trademarks and are the property of their respective owners.

This is a work of fiction. Names, characters, places, and incidents either are the product of the author's imagination or are used fictitiously. Any resemblance to actual persons, living or dead, is entirely coincidental.

for Alexandra and Elise

Chapter 1

GYMBOS

I don't blame them for feeling suspicious. I blame them for acting so damn obvious about it.

From my squishy fitness mat, I ease into a quad stretch and can't help but laugh as I watch a gymbo (gym bimbo, a species easily identified by its high ponytail and its brightly patterned, overpriced, skin-tight fitness apparel) cautiously stow her precious belongings in an unlocked locker before starting her workout. She tries to play it off, looking over her shoulder nonchalantly like she's tossing her ponytail back and adjusting her hot pink shoelaces, but it's so obvious she's really looking to see if anyone sinister is watching her slip her iPad Air into the little unlocked cubby.

A secure mind doesn't need to look over its shoulder. If I were the cheeky and sociable kind, I'd walk right over and tell her "You're not fooling anyone, honey; lock that shit up." But I'm not. I'm pretty sure I've never even been sociable enough for anyone to call me cheeky. In all fairness to the gymbo, I don't have much faith in the patrons of the Percival O'Shaughnessy Community Center either, even if they are a bunch of salt-of-the-earth Johnson County suburbanites with double jogging strollers and e-reader cases that color coordinate with their Nike running shorts.

Of course, it's hard for me to have faith in the innate morality of anyone else when I'm the one who's watching them leave their crap unprotected so I can take it home with me. Anyone *could* just walk up and take it, but I actually do. Why do these gym rats just leave their stuff unguarded? Why aren't there surveillance cameras that protect these provincial Percival O'Shaughnessy Community Center patrons from theft? More to the point, how do I get away with it?

I ask myself these questions every time I enter this place, and even answer them in the same order (not just because I'm a tad obsessive-compulsive in addition to being a kleptomaniac within the walls of this building). Why does everyone just leave their valuables strewn about willy-nilly? Your guess is as good as mine. Maybe they really do believe in the innate goodness of humanity. Maybe they're just lazy. Maybe they forgot their locker combinations. Who knows?

Why aren't there surveillance cameras? Well, this isn't exactly an expensive, elite training facility that would be the envy of a professional football team (or even the Kansas City Chiefs). This is the Percival O'-Fucking-Shaughnessy Community Center, funded by the good taxpaying people of Johnson County, Kansas, and people like me who pay thirty bucks a month to swim in the same piss-infested lap pool they use to give swimming lessons to six-year-olds. Besides, old man Percy (the guy whose long-ass name is on the side of the building) is a paranoid nut job who isn't big on being Big Brother. He still comes here to work out every once in a while, and by work out, I mean turtle walk around the indoor track in his double-knit polyester pants and Velcro shoes.

And of course, the million-dollar question: how do I get away with it? This may sound trite, but it's easier than you might think. I actually do just walk up, acting completely unsuspicious, and take what I want. Like the guy I read about who strolled into a Sears, slapped a "Sold" tag on a piano, and rolled it right out of there. They say the clerks even held the door open for him. The principle is very much the same with random crap at the POS Community Center, and a lot easier to carry out than a piano.

It also doesn't hurt that I am a proverbial plain Jane when it comes to looks and I have the most boring name on the planet. No one's going to suspect Ann Josephson of stealing; she's in here all the time. And I am, six days a week, sometimes more. Even when I'm not physically here, I'm still metaphysically here. My name's on the indoor triathlon results sheet, my face is one of many in last summer's poorly named bikini challenge (or as I called it, bikini-challenged) finish line photo, and my fitness statistics are on the Community Center leader board for the year. Yep, I can pretty much get away with anything, and no one is going to suspect me.

Take today, for example. Today is Tuesday. I know this because the maintenance staff is setting up the volleyball nets for tonight's league game, step aerobics is starting on the other side of the partition, and the soccer moms looking to shake the baby weight (can you still call it baby weight if your kids are old enough to play soccer?) are filing in for 7:30 Zumba. This also means that it's a counter-clockwise day for the indoor track. On clockwise days, you can walk the track and the lockers up here will never be out of your eye line, but on counterclockwise days, the wall against which these lockers are mounted makes a pretty sweet blind spot (sweet for me, anyway). The only way you'll be able to constantly keep an eye on your stuff is to look behind you, but nobody likes to look behind themselves when they're walking the track. It makes the people walking behind them uncomfortable and makes the walker look insecure. Like I said, a secure mind doesn't need to look over its shoulder.

I'm sufficiently stretched out, so I begin a steady jog around the track, dodging oversized-stroller-pushers and indolent grannies. Sounds float up to greet me as I steady my pace. Sneakers chirp against one half of the basketball court, the half they're using for volleyball tonight. Weights clink together between reps on the lat machine as a grunt-lifter checks his form in the mirror. It's the grunter's symphony: grunt, clink, grunt, clink. From the other half of the track, the step aerobics instructor starts the peppy remix medley of Rihanna, starting with "Only Girl in the World." They use it every week; it's a wonder the CD still plays. Through the wall of foggy windows that separate the impressive pool area from the rest of the gym, children shriek with delight as the water slide transports them to the lazy river below, their eyes red from piss and chlorine. From the open door to the Chiefs room (they named all the studios after Kansas City–area sports teams) where Zumba's about to begin, they're playing "Country Roads," of all things. I don't know that I could pull a less Latin-inspired song out of my ass if I tried, but there's no accounting for taste. Then finally, there's the ambient tinny buzz of the tunes that leak out of other people's headphones as I pass them on the track.

I rarely listen to my own music when I exercise. For most people, working out is the thing they do to block out the rest of the world. For me, it's pretty much the only way I am a part of it. By the time the last straggler shuffles into the Chiefs room for Zumba, "Country Roads" has been replaced by something more maraca-fied and I've already clocked eight and a half laps on the track, which I know from memory (and the sign on the wall) is a mile on the outermost lane. Sometimes—when I'm not dodging a ton of other people on a packed Tuesday evening—I like to close my eyes and make my way around the track just to see if I can orient myself based on sound and feeling alone. I like it best when I can match the noises to the people, the people who don't see me, the person right in front of their eyes.

I know my own pace and how many steps there are between each turn. I let my eyelids fall closed as I round a corner, the visible length of track in front of me clear of other people. To my left, I can hear the solo racquetball player who comes in here every day at 7 p.m. like clockwork, and has great taste in music, according to the iPod Nano of his I have sitting in my room of stolen goods at home, a room which I affectionately refer to as "Room 403," after the "forbidden" HTTP response code, because I'm just that much of a dork. When I hear the water fountain, the one next to the handicapped restroom, I am reminded of how thirsty running these two miles and change has made me, and that Zumba is about to be dismissed. I open my eyes and slow my pace to a trot so I can stop for a drink at my favorite water fountain, the one where the water comes out colder than all the others, but not before stopping off at the cubby lockers to have a peek inside.

I don't see anything that really interests me in the lockers. There's the iPad Air the gymbo left, but I already have six of those. There's a brand new twelve-pack of Asics running socks that are mighty tempting, since they are my favorite brand of fitness socks, but they're various shades of bright pink, which is not my color. Come to think of it, I don't think it's anyone over the age of ten's color. I shrug it off and continue over to the fountain, the sound of Zumba closing applause at my back. Why do people clap for an instructor after a class, anyway?

I bend over the mega-cold water so I can watch the gymbos out of the corner of my eye. As I drink, I smell a hint of something that's vaguely familiar but hard to pinpoint. Maybe it reminds me of one of the Scentsy bars my mother keeps dumping on me by the box full—she shills for all those multilevel marketing rackets and pawns all the stuff she doesn't like on me, all under the guise of being magnanimous. Zeppelin, maybe, part of the "for men" collection but still one my favorites—so much so that I'm pretty sure I committed the product description to memory. ". . . composed of notes of refreshing citrus, green sage, herbaceous vetiver (which I don't think is an actual thing), and earthy sandalwood." Yes, that's definitely it, minus whatever vetiver is.

I follow the scent down to its source, a hunter-green zip-up cardigan—too big for me—carelessly tossed under the water fountain for safekeeping. I find the manly yet soft scent intoxicating even though I would never wear it myself. It certainly smells better than I do right now, a thin layer of salty sweat plastered to my skin like aerosol sunscreen. I like the jacket—its smell and its color though not its size, but two out of three ain't bad. I tie it around my waist, waving to Jeanette at the front desk as I walk out and head home.

Chapter 2

THE SEAGULLS AND THE RESOLUTIONARIES

I t makes me sad that Christmas comes but once a year, but not because of good cheer or magical Santa dust or anything. At the Percival O'Shaughnessy Community Center, it truly is a time of peace and goodwill. The heavenly week between Christmas and New Year's, I could have taken up all three swim lanes by myself if I'd felt so inclined, could have even backstroked with my eyes closed and willingly drifted into the blue-and-white lane dividers blanketed with a thin, permanent layer of green mildew. The only sound was my own stroke-stroke-stroking as my freckled arms hit the water, no ear-splitting screams of children splashing violently in the un-roped section of the lap pool, no Lady Gaga blasting from the boombox of the blonde, tan Shawnee Mission North high school sophomore who lifeguards on Mondays. So few people find the time to squeeze in a workout between around-the-clock holiday meals, it's even been hard to steal any-thing these days . . . but somehow I manage. I've been watching my *Washington Journal* episodes on C-SPAN on the communal treadmill TV and not a single person has scoffed in disgust and changed the channel, like they do the rest of the year.

By contrast, I thank all of the gods (just to make sure all my bases are covered) that January only comes once a year. All the peace and quiet of the Christmas season goes right out the window as the resolutionaries come out of the woodwork and flood every square foot of the community center. January third is the worst. I don't know why everyone waits two days to start their "new year, new you" regimen, but they do. Coincidentally, today is January third. I should have known better than to brave the gym on this least solemn of days; I had to park at the bank across the street since the community center parking lot was full of shiny Chevy Tahoes with stick families emblazoned on their back windshields.

I could've walked here instead of bitching about having to park so far away. My apartment is only five or six blocks from the Percy; it's part of why I'm in here so often (that, and the com-pulsion, the routine, and the boredom). In my defense, though, it's January and it's cold as balls out there. We won't see the sun peek out from these depressing gray clouds the entire month, and there's this sad layer of snow that won't quite go away, but collects at the side of the road in brown sludgy piles and in ran-dom patches on everyone's lawn that leave everything soggy. It only takes me two minutes to drive in my warm car to get here. In the fifteen minutes it would take me to walk here through this winter blunderland scene trying to cross streets that were clearly not designed with pedestrians in mind, I'd want to blow my brains out with a Nerf gun.

There is a long line to punch in, since most of the people in front of me haven't used their gym access codes since last January. Jeanette at the front desk is frantically looking up people by their addresses while an elderly community center volunteer I don't recognize handles all the changes of address, information updates, and other nonsense that people wait to do until January third, the single most inconvenient day of the year. I shoot imaginary lasers through the backs of people's fur-lined hood–covered heads as I impatiently shiver in line. My access code is muscle memory by this point. I could recite it if I were looking at the keypad, but it would take me three times as long to recite it as it takes me to punch it in.

By the time I punch in and grumble up the stairs, I see that the seagulls have attacked the stretching area. Seagulls are the people who come in here after an eleven-month hiatus, groan loudly as they stretch out (since their muscles haven't experienced it in almost an entire year), then pull out all the resistance bands, medicine balls, foam rollers, yoga mats, steps, and free weights they can only to leave them strewn about everywhere like the aftermath of Christmas morning. I call them seagulls because they fly in, make a lot of noise, shit all over everything, and then fly away. Why should they care that they're leaving everything a sweaty, incomprehensible mess for the long series of people after them? They'll be gone by Valentine's Day anyway.

I spend a good eight minutes running gym wipes over the equipment and putting everything back in its assigned place while I wait for an elliptical to free up. Some of us actually do care about the money and time we put into coming here. It's not just the ellipticals that are all taken; it's the recumbent bikes, treadmills, the stair climbers - everything. Begrudgingly, I decide to run on the indoor track again, dodging the slow women with jogging strollers who are apparently unable to read signs that indicate the lanes they're supposed to use. It sure is a good thing genies aren't real, because in January, I pretty much wish everyone around me would disappear.

I know what you're thinking—I should really be salivating with joy because the gym would now be full of new people to steal from, newly obtained toys to take home and add to Room 403. Nope. My salivation level is completely normal. My therapist could probably explain it better than I can (I have to go once every two weeks otherwise my parents refuse to help cover my rent), but I just don't have the desire to take something from these people who have no respect for this place where I spend the better part of my week.

The more laps I make around the track, the angrier I get, which is annoying, since exercise is pretty much the only way I can feel good about myself. I decide to cut my workout short and head down the stairs to the women's locker room, just in time to get stuck behind a woman with two asses trying desperately not to fall down the stairs. Noodle legs—I know them well but I haven't experienced them in a very long time, probably because I come here more often than every January.

There's a line for the showers, a line that consists of a gaggle of overweight women huddling behind threadbare towels that fit nicely into a compact gym bag but barely conceal their collective backs and fronts. No, thanks. I will just shower at home. I worked up more of a sweat trying to disintegrate these people with my mind than I did jogging the track, anyway. Scattered valuables litter the benches in front of my locker, which I of course secure with a purple Master combination lock. (Rumor has it there's a thief around here.) Despite the fact that I'm far too annoyed to want to steal anything, a fabulous pair of red high heels hooked expertly on the edge of the bench catch my eye. I have very few occasions that necessitate shoes that are not of the flip-flop or cross-trainer variety, but then I also have very few shoes for said few occasions. I pick up the right one, not caring who's watching—like I said, all you have to do is act like it's yours and no one is the wiser; people are a lot less perceptive than we give them credit for. Unfortunately for me, it's a size too big, so I nonchalantly return it to its spot, hoisting my bag over my shoulder and squeezing through the crowd.

"Hey Ann," Jeanette says to me as I try to sneak out without making small talk. I like Jeanette, definitely more than I like the other desk jockeys here. Jeanette had a particular glow in her eye tonight; maybe it's left over from that date she had last week, the one I know about because I stole her day planner two days ago.

"Hey. Crazy night, right?" I'm almost cut off by the terrified screams of a curly-haired child in the nursery next to the front desk.

Jeanette sighs loudly. "It's January, all right. But hey, we've had a record number of new memberships this week."

They have a record number of new memberships every January. "Eh. They'll thin out eventually."

"I sure hope not," Jeanette says, twisting a bracelet around her left wrist. New. Sparkly. "But you're probably right."

"See you tomorrow?" I smile, pulling on my gloves. Stupid cold weather.

Jeanette nods. I turn to leave when I hear her voice behind me. "Oh hey, did you see?"

"See what?" Why is my skin already crawling? I didn't take the shoes. I didn't take anything.

"This year's catalog!" She reaches under the desk and withdraws the Percival O'Shaughnessy Community Center 2016 Class and Activities Catalog. On the cover, my own determined face stares back at me, running the indoor relay in my favorite sports bra. I feel my jaw drop.

"I'm on the catalog?" I don't mean for it to come out like a question.

"Mmhmm."

"And everyone gets these?"

"Everyone in the city."

"Great." I lie. *Super. Now I can really blend in.* "See you tomorrow."

I turn to leave, my mind racing and the familiar tug in my gut wrenching its way to the surface. I must find something to steal before I can leave. If I don't, the wrenching will only grow until I am shaking from anxiety and eating everything in my fridge. The only thing between me and the door is the "adult lounge," which is really more of a conference room where they have AA meetings twice a week and old people congregate to watch Fox News and drink shitty coffee. I pop in and glance around. It doesn't even have to be something good. It just has to be something. Something that isn't mine. I feel my pulse regulate as I spot a coffee mug with a bright red smear of lipstick on the rim sitting next to the sink. It's a pretty brazen shade for a suburban queen, almost the exact color of the shoes in the locker room. Maybe they belong to the same person. Maybe the match is intentional. Maybe she came straight to the gym after seducing her pool boy. Do people have their pool boys over in January?

I admit I am impressed. I'd never have the guts to wear this color lipstick. I awkwardly stuff the mug into my coat pocket and can't wait to add it to Room 403 when I get home.

Chapter 3

SKINNY BITCH

By the time I make it home, my temporary hyperventilation after the community center catalog unveiling is a distant memory, albeit it's a short distance. As much I want to believe I recovered from my little episode with remarkable aplomb, I have yet to make it any farther than barely inside my front door. It's currently propping me up as I sit, slumped against it on my dingy, worn-out carpet. I stare at the red ring of lipstick on the coffee mug I just stole. I have more coffee mugs than I could ever drink out of myself; what made me think I needed another one? Even as I ask myself–silently, I think–I know the answer. It was there; that's all. Nothing more. A gesture as empty as the dirty mug in my hand, as empty as I feel sitting on the floor of the two-bedroom apartment I said I needed for office space.

My mother likes to remind me that pity parties should never last more than thirty seconds, so I take a deep breath and make myself get up from the floor and walk across the expanse of the apartment to the second bedroom, Room 403, the one that isn't being used for office space. Instead, it's where the mass of things I have stolen from people at the community center form a mountain of junk that reaches to the broken ceiling fan I can't possibly ask the maintenance guys to fix without being reported to the Health Department. I pause with my hand on the doorknob, reminding myself to breathe before I twist it open with a quiet creak.

I don't even feel the tears of shame as the junk mountain comes into view, I'm so accustomed to them every time I come in here, an instant reminder of what a pathetic human being I am. I hurl the coffee mug at the mountain, hoping it will shatter upon impact, but it lands on the dark green cardigan I stole last week, which softens the blow just enough to let it roll down to the bottom of the pile without incident. I wipe my eyes on my sweaty sleeves, transfixed on the cardigan, and then pick it up and bury my face in it. It still smells like the Zeppelin Scentsy bar. I lower it just below my eyes, only enough to keep from running into the walls as I turn and leave Room 403 and toss it on the well-made duvet cover in my own bedroom, pristinely clean by comparison. My own sweaty clothes I toss on the floor before I step in the shower and let the water warm as I stand under it.

"I can't stop. I can't stop. I can't stop," I hear myself repeating, though I'm not sure when I started saying it. I try to remember my therapist's advice to clear my head: take ten deep breaths, count each one out loud. By the time I get to six, I can feel my heart rate returning to a semi-normal level and I imagine the shower washing all the anxiety off me with the layer of salty body odor.

I don't bother drying my hair before throwing myself on the bed with an audible thud. I hug the cardigan to my chest and squeeze my eyes shut, envisioning the kind of man who would wear the dark green color, the woodsy masculine fragrance, imagining him lying next to me, telling me everything is going to be all right. In my mind, he has curly dishwater blonde hair and a single dimple on the right side of his perfect smile, a smile my dentist father would approve of. I never said it had to make sense. At least it's slightly less pathetic than a man-shaped body pillow.

When I am still wide awake after twenty minutes, I decide to get up and do some work. Willing myself out of my comfy bed doesn't make me feel better, but it at least makes me feel like I might manage to be less of a garbage human for one day. I slip on a tank top and a pair of lounge pants (which I refer to as happy pants) before sliding my naked arms through the sleeves of the cardigan as if I were wearing my boyfriend's shirt. It nearly hangs to my knees.

I have thirteen messages on eLance. It's easy enough to get work on there for a freelance graphic designer. The pay's usually shit by comparison, since you're competing with graphic designers in parts of the world where six dollars an hour goes a lot further, but it sure beats going to an office for eight hours a day just so people can tell you to make the font bigger and create logos that look sort of like Apple, but are most definitely *not* Apple. People always say they want Apple-like design, then bristle at all the negative space before listing out all the things that could fill it. I start at the top of my unread inbox. The subject lines read something like this:

Can we make font bigger?
Need new logo. Think Apple but not Apple.
Rec'd final invoice
Re: bigger font?
Modern logo requested
Waiting for final invoice

Because they often don't pay much (or pay much attention), it's pretty easy to get away with going past the originally agreed upon deadline. They almost expect it out of creatives. I usually don't have more than about six small jobs up in the air at one time, most of which I knock out in a couple of hours when I feel like working—when I feel like I do now. I begrudgingly biggify some fonts, bang out a couple of logos, send some invoices, make some PayPal withdrawals, send some follow-ups and thank-yous, and rate some employer profiles, but only manage to kill about four hours. On the bright side, I don't feel like I'm being sucked into a pit of despair anymore, which is always a plus. I calculate my month-to-date earnings; I only need a couple more jobs this month to pay the handful of bills I have. My parents still think they need to help pay my rent, and I'm not about to tell them to stop or take on more work than I can handle just to let them off the hook. They spend more per month on their stupid country club membership; they can afford it.

I unzip and shove my hands into the warm pockets of the cardigan, surprised when my fingertips feel something hard and cold. I recognize it as an iPhone before I can even bring it up out of the pocket. I look at it, the logo on the back exactly like Apple. I flip it over and try to turn it on, but the battery's dead. I retrieve one of the many iThing chargers I have at arm's length and plug it into the USB of the computer I use for work. The device's name is Susan, a taskbar balloon tells me. The screen comes to life after a couple minutes, but it's passcode protected. I try 1-2-3-4, in the event the phone belongs to a complete bonehead, but alas it does not. The numeric code for Susan doesn't work either, and after a few more basic permutations, I find I feel just as shitty as I did before I dug myself out of my pit of despair by getting some work done. Instead, I flip off the monitor and fall into bed without removing the cardigan, falling instantly asleep to the almost imperceptible smell of sandalwood.

I don't wake up until the next day at 11:00 a.m., which makes me feel even worse. I resolve to go to the gym and, just this once, refrain from stealing anything. Not even a stupid goddamn coffee mug.

The treadmills are the only machines available at the gym, so even though my last two workouts were runs, I begrudgingly go for a repeat performance. Just in case I couldn't feel worse about myself, Skinny Bitch sidles up on the treadmill beside me three minutes into my run. I call her Skinny Bitch because I assume she wants everyone to know both how skinny and how much of a bitch she is. We all know she is skinny because she chooses to do her workouts in a white sports bra that sets off her unnaturally tanned skin and allows the better part of her gigantic boobs to spill over the top like a Renaissance festival corset. It also exposes what might be the flattest tummy I have ever seen on a real human being. Like, maddeningly flat. I'd like to think that if I had a belly that flat I would show it off, too, but even being in here every day has yet to do that for me. Besides, my sports bra is about the color of her skin, and my skin is about the color of her sports bra. No sense in blinding everyone and showing off how well-used my sports bra is. Okay, I might just be projecting the bitchy part, but Skinny Bitch has a better ring to it than Skinny Fake Baker Trollface.

I picture "Sexy and I Know It" theme music playing her in everywhere she goes. And she totally is, in my completely asexual opinion. Typically, she pairs the white sports bra with an equally white pair of yoga pants patently reserved for people who don't need yoga. I look around the gym, partly because I think I might be staring (which she's probably used to but doesn't make it any less creepy) and partly to see if there's any female in the building who could pull off the white yoga pants like she does. There isn't—myself included. Today, however, she's donning a pair of hot pink running shorts that barely cover her ass and reveal thighs that I'd swear were airbrushed if I weren't looking at them in real life right now. Skinny bitches like her are why people hate coming to the gym. Shit, I must be staring again.

"You got a problem?" she says before taking a sip of water from her color-coordinated hot pink water bottle.

Yes, I am insanely jealous of your nonexistent tummy, thigh gap, and enormous tits. "No," I say, forcing a smile and dropping my gaze, only to realize she probably wears the long white yoga pants not only to show off how good she looks in them, but also to cover the ankle monitor strapped around her left leg. I better stop staring; who knows what kind of temper she has. She may be skinny, but she's probably pretty scrappy, and the last fight I was in was in third grade and ended with a tetherball to the face. My face, not fellow third grader Carrie Schmidt's.

I tick my treadmill pace up to 5.2 miles per hour (my normal distance running stride) and change the channel on the TV in between myself and Skinny Bitch from ESPN to CSPAN with the controls on the treadmill. I can't help but notice when she ticks hers up to 5.3 and changes the channel on the same TV to one of those Real Housewives of Wherever shows on the E! channel. "Entertainment Television" my milky white ass.

Two can play at this game. I go to 5.5, my stride getting choppier. She doesn't relent, making a show of going to 5.7, not even a glimmer of sweat on her décolletage. I remind myself not to stare, but wonder out of the corner of my eye how anyone's tits can remain inhumanly stationary like hers. Even my modest B-cups are starting to cry uncle with each passing bounce.

I like to think that I win, because she stops her treadmill and dabs at the invisible sweat on her forehead before turning on her ankle-monitored heel and walking away without wiping the machine down. I know she didn't drip sweat all over it because she apparently does not have sweat glands like a normal human being, but it's the principle of the thing. You use a piece of community equipment, you wipe it down when you're done, even if it you don't use it long enough to get your heart rate up.

"Don't worry," says a deep voice belonging to a not wholly unhandsome man who at some point materialized on the treadmill to my right, jarring me away from my thought circus. "You're way hotter than she is."

"And you're a really shitty liar." The words immediately spill out of my mouth before I have a chance to realize I am saying them out loud and reel them back in.

Chapter 4

BLUECIFER

"What did you say?" the guy on the treadmill next to me says between loud, cackling bouts of laughter. I struggle to recall if I actually said the words, or if I just thought them loudly enough that he read my brain phrases telepathically. I couldn't have said it out loud; I don't willingly engage in conversation with other people

Shit. "Me? Nothing." I say, feeling the lie bring all the blood in my body rushing to my cheeks, which I am sure are now a shade of red reserved for the goriest of horror movies or coffee mug lipstick.

"I believe you just called me a shitty liar. You're one to talk," he says, rivulets of sweat dripping from his dark hairline, showing the earliest hints of receding. *Please tell me this is not your typical look for hitting on women,* I think to myself, followed by *please don't hear my inner thoughts.* He's not what I'd call unattractive, but not exactly a head-turner either. I'd give him a solid 5.5. Nothing wrong with being slightly above-average looking. It helps with the blending in.

"I'm sorry," I say.

"That's quite all right. You're entitled to your opinion. And not the first one to accuse me of being the world's worst liar."

"I didn't say you were the world's worst liar. I said you're a shitty liar."

"Oh, so now you admit it? So much perjury in so little time."

"I said I was sorry," I say, starting to reach for my earbuds and the volume control, universal body language for "shut the fuck up and leave me alone."

"I see you in here a lot," he says, interrupting my body speech mid-sentence.

I wonder what he's implying, which could range anywhere from "I've noticed you sometimes adjust the ass elastic on your bathing suit between laps" to "I've noticed you have an affinity for pilfering shit from people's unsecured lockers." I don't know which is worse. Judging from the goofy grin on his sweat-beaded face, I'm inclined to think the former, but I can't be sure. Then again, since I am in here ninety-two percent of the days in the year, could be I just landed a blip spot on his proverbial radar. In which case, astute observation there, Captain Obvious.

"Yep."

"You ever here on Thursday nights?"

Only when I have a pulse, and when I'm not reheating spaghetti on Thanksgiving Day. "Yep."

"You ever watch the dodgeball games?"

"Yep." League dodgeball night is one of my favorite nights, as it so happens. Most of the dodgeballers aren't community center members so they just leave their crap in a wadded pile in the lobby, practically begging to be stolen. But I don't tell him that.

"Ever think about joining?"

"Nope."

"Ah, she does say something besides 'Yep.'"

Sure do, numbnuts. I smile as politely as I can. I nearly yell to imply the volume in my headphones is much higher than it really is, "I'm going to watch my show now."

"*Washington Journal* is 'your show'?" he returns the incline on his treadmill to zero.

"I happen to find it fascinating. This is what reality television is supposed to be. Not a bunch of artificial drama about stuff that doesn't even matter, like who can make the best quiche lorraine or turn a profit on investment properties using only faux marble countertops." *Or who has the fakest boobs.*

"Hey, I'm not judging," he says, wiping his face with a once-white gym towel as he pushes the COOL DOWN button. I glare. "Okay, I'm judging a little. Anyway, one of the gals on our dodgeball team just found out she's expecting, so she's bowing out for the rest of the season. Any chance you'd be interested in filling in for her?"

"Sorry, I think that's the night 'Q&A with Richard Baker' is on."

"You know they re-air that all the time on C-SPAN 2, right?"

I've got to give it to the guy, at least he has a clue what he's talking about. Then again, he could know just as much about the Thursday night wedding reality show lineup on TLC. People are always watching that in here. I think for a second. Let's see . . . a team sport, with other people, most of whom I have probably stolen from, who expect me to do silly things like throw a weight-less foam ball with some semblance of aim, catch balls flying at my face, and somehow manage to gracefully dodge these flying balls without falling on my face? I think I'd rather spend my Thursday night babysitting a teething toddler with diarrhea.

"I don't think that's really my thing, but thanks for asking."

He puts up an arm in acknowledgement. "Fair enough. I'll probably ask again, so don't forget this conversation. You'll be here, right?"

Fuck you. "Probably."

He walks away, and my eyes follow him as he returns with the little gym wipes every person with half a soul should use when they sweat as much as he does on a machine that will invariably be claimed by another gym patron within seconds. At least that's one point in his favor. After he wipes down his own machine, he repeats the action on the treadmill next to him. Two points in his favor. For all I know, he could be a psycho killer, but at least he does more than his part to keep the cardio equipment germ-free. A chubby older woman takes his place on the treadmill before he can turn the corner to the exit stairs.

So, someone does notice the fact that I occupy time and space. As a human with feelings, I should probably be pleased. As a human with a vagina, I should be a gushy mess. As a human with a compulsion, however, this is very, very bad. The last thing I need is for some big dumb man to be watching my every move while I do my one of my workouts, which as I look down at the treadmill display I see has now spanned forty-five minutes. Probably time to get of the treadmill, to clear my head if nothing else. I'd wipe down the machine that Skinny Bitch neglected to, but some poor unsuspecting community center patron has already staked her claim, and has been stretching her legs on it for the past three minutes. Maybe sometime this century she'll actually use it.

I start to walk toward the exit, but I can't help but notice that the seagulls have attacked the stretching area again. This time, there are resistance bands, lightweight dumbbells, yoga mats, and medicine balls so randomly dispersed that I can't even walk through it in a straight line.

My face flushes with frustration. I grab a bucket of gym wipes and start methodically wiping down all the askew items and returning them to their proper places, going over and over the conversation with the treadmill gentleman, whose name I realize I never learned, in my now-throbbing head. I'm sure I've seen him before, but I don't think I've ever knowingly stolen from him, so maybe it really was just innocent conversation. Then again, I've had so few casual and innocent conversations in the last few years that I don't even know if he was hitting on me or was really just that desperate for a warm body in decent shape for his dodgeball team.

Why *wouldn't* he ask me? If he is half as observant as he appeared, he must have seen my indoor triathlon stats posted by the front desk and my picture on the 2016 catalog and put two and two together. Are normal people that observant? They certainly don't seem to be, or else I wouldn't be able to get away with the shit I do. Who the hell is this guy, and why does he seem so interested in me? I suck at being invisible, apparently, when all this time I thought being invisible was just about the only thing I'm good at.

The last thing I neatly stack in its proper place is the foam roller I lovingly nicknamed Bluecifer back when I was using it for physical therapy on my IT band injury.

"We meet again, old friend," I quietly say to the swirly blue foam cylinder as I methodically wipe it down, knowing full well that I might appear psychotic to innocent passersby, having a more comfortable conversation with a piece of gym equipment than the one I just had with a fellow human being. Maybe my therapist is right, I really do suck at forming meaningful relationships with other people. I'm paraphrasing of course. Therapists aren't supposed to tell you you suck at anything, even if you do. Like I do at team sports, carrying on a normal conversation, and being invisible. Bluecifer was a pretty good friend, all things considered, inflicting physical pain to make me feel physically better, which I suppose would make me a masochist.

In my own mind, I have lots of friends, they just don't happen to know we're friends or that I know who all their emergency contacts and lunch appointments are with, because I steal their day planners. Day planners are kind of a guilty pleasure, but they're the best way to get inside someone's psyche other than an iPhone without an unlock sequence. The newly acquired one is waiting for me at home, just begging to be cracked so I can figure out the man behind the Zeppelin-scented cardigan.

I'm already pulling out of the parking lot when I realize that I was so wrapped up in my own thoughts I didn't even steal anything.

Chapter 5

CDO

The only person besides me who knows about my stuff-stealing is my therapist, but I significantly downplay it in our sessions and she has a nicer name for it: context-specific compulsive kleptomania. I've seen a therapist regularly since I was twelve, not because I've needed one since then, but because my parents enjoy being conspicuous consumers of socially progressive ideals. They thought it would be a good idea back then, and they view it as a necessary condition for paying the better part of my living expenses now. Some weeks, this hour is the only verbal conversation I have with someone other than myself or with the stuff in room 403.

My therapist's office is in one of those dime-a-dozen complexes that are always advertising space available for lease. Beige walls, gray carpets, nondescript suite numbers and nameplates. For anyone who didn't know better, they might mistake the office of "Andrea Kelley, LCSW" for a dermatologist or an estate

attorney, particularly since she shares a hallway with two derma-
tologists and two estate attorneys.

I walk through the door to suite 202 for my regular bi-weekly
appointment at 1:00 p.m. on Wednesday, the same time I could
be enjoying Zumba or observing senior aquarobics class from
a distance at the community center. Dr. Kelley (please, call me
Andrea) greets me instead of Veronica, her receptionist. Maybe
she's off at Zumba. As usual, Dr. Kelley is hastily finishing a lunch
of Subway six-inch tuna salad, emanating an unpleasant aroma
that doesn't exactly make me want to talk about my thoughts
and feelings. I can attest to the fact that she eats the same lunch
every Wednesday, and I suspect every day (I've noticed Dr. Kelley has a very special brand of OCD; it could easily be called
CDO—like OCD, but the letters are in alphabetical order like
they should be).

She ushers me as usual into her office and motions for me to
sit on the yellow IKEA couch with a box of tissues resting on the
arm, one I am proud to say I have never touched.

"So, Ann," she asks me, a yellow legal pad resting on her
crossed legs, "how's your week been? How are you coming in
today?" This is her typical ice breaker. I guess it would be in
poor taste to start our session off with, "have you stolen anything
particularly interesting this week?"

"Fine." My usual answer to her usual ice breaker.

She purses her already thin lips and begins scribbling on the
legal pad. "Have you been to the community center this week?"

"Every day but today," I answer. I find it's easier to just tell
the truth in these sessions, even if it is my own version of the
truth, otherwise I'm just wasting my parents' money and my
own time. I'm not a terrible liar, like the treadmill dude I talked
to yesterday, but if I never talk to people, I never have to lie.

Thinking back to the conversation with the treadmill guy makes my face feel flushed. I hope it's not noticeable.

"Was there something especially different about this week?" she asks with a knowing side-eye.

So much for not being noticeable. "Not really," I say. It's not that much of a truth-stretch. All I did was talk to someone. That's normal, right?

"Not really? Nothing different at all? You went in, worked out, stole something that belonged to someone else, and left like every other day?" I can see her drawing boxes on the legal pad, slowly enough to make the corners nice and square. It's what she does. OCD.

"Not every day, no. Actually I think you'd be proud of me," I say, sitting up straighter as though what I'm about to say warrants a medal or a cookie. "Yesterday I went to the gym for almost two hours and didn't steal a thing."

"Why not?"

Because I'm totes normal. "I guess I forgot to."

"Something must have occupied your thoughts to make you forget." She's still working on her doodle boxes with perfect ninety-degree angles.

Damn you and your perfectly-aligned framed diplomas. I shrug in response.

"Tell me what happened yesterday at the gym," she says.

I sigh audibly before launching in. "Well, there was this perfect-looking woman—I mean, like, infuriatingly perfect-looking—on the treadmill next to mine. She kept trying to outdo me and kept changing the channel on me. I got annoyed and pushed myself pretty hard until she left." I sigh.

"Then this knucklehead on the other treadmill next to mine tells me I'm hotter than the bimbo who just left, which was a pretty obvious lie."

"And you told him that?"

Damn skippy. "I-I didn't mean to; it just kind of came out."

"And then you had a pleasant conversation with this . . . knucklehead?"

"I guess so—maybe not pleasant, but a conversation."

"So, what did you two talk about?"

"I don't know. Stuff."

"Come on, Ann. You're wasting my time and yours by hedging. What kind of stuff?"

"Going to the community center. C-SPAN. He wants me to join his team for the dodgeball league."

"He said that?"

I nod, averting her uncomfortable scrutinizing gaze.

"Are you going to join?"

I'm having trouble deciding which activity I might despise more—this session, or joining the dodgeball league. "No, I don't think so."

"Why not?"

"It's not really my thing."

"Not really your thing because it would put you too close to the people you ordinarily steal from?"

I don't say anything, but I don't have to. She already knows the answer.

"Let's put this dodgeball business aside for a moment. Let's go back to this conversation with the gentleman. How long did the two of you talk?"

"Well, it was right when I started my cool down on the treadmill, so about ten minutes."

"Where were his things during this conversation?"

I close my eyes to visualize. "Against the back wall of the cardio room in a pile on the floor."

"And what did he have in his pile of things?"

"Not much, just his keys, a wallet, and a warm jacket."

"Did you consider taking these things?"

"No."

"Why not?"

Because without his keys he couldn't have gotten away from me. "I don't know. I guess I didn't need those things and he did."

"Ann," she says, narrowing her gaze at me. "You know full well you don't need any of the things you steal from people. You don't steal out of necessity." She initiates one of those long periods of silence designed specifically to get me to say what I'm really thinking, though I suspect she wouldn't really want to hear my inner thoughts even if she could.

"I just didn't feel like I should steal from him. It didn't occur to me that I could."

"When's the last time you talked to someone in the gym, a conversation like this one?"

"I don't know. It's been a while."

She sits back in her chair and looks at me intently. "For some time now, I've suspected that the reason you take things from other people is because you feel it's the only way you can form a connection with them. People need connections. You lack the ability to connect with other people and this is how your subconscious makes up for those connections. When you steal an object from the other person, it's how you interact with them and get to know them. In this incident, you had an *actual* connection with someone else and as a result, you didn't feel the need to steal from that person. You got to know a little bit about who that person was and it satisfied your compulsion to steal. Do you think that makes sense?"

I shrug indifferently. "I don't know."

"I'm going ask you to challenge yourself this week. When are the dodgeball games?"

"Thursday nights, between six and nine."

"Go play just one game with this team. If after playing it, you find out that it's really not your thing, then you can choose to never go back and I won't think any less of you or ask you to do it again."

"What if I really don't want to?" I ask, shifting uncomfortably on the creaking vinyl sofa.

She sets the legal pad on the desk behind her and leans forward, placing her crossed arms on her crossed legs. "What if you do?"

Chapter 6

AVERAGE JOE

It's Saturday, which is leg day for me, and the middle-aged gentleman on the weight machine next to me is wearing jeans. If it were up to me, I'd have one of the new POS Community Center security guards I hear they've hired put on specially made Stormtrooper uniforms and escort anyone entering the gym area in jeans to the nearest exit. I'd also create a special circle of hell for the same people. Unfortunately, it isn't within my power to do either of those things, so I just sit, try not to watch, and imagine how unpleasant it must be to perform squats. The swamp-ass factor alone makes me shudder at the thought.

I think back to the first time they made me change out of my jeans for gym class. I must have been twelve or so, just entering junior high. Granted, I hated gym class then, but I pretty much hated everything because I was a twelve-year-old girl, and twelve-year-old girls are a despicable class of humans full of hormones, awkwardness, and loathing. I'm not saying I would slap my twelve-year-old self if I crossed her on the sidewalk today or anything, but we probably wouldn't hang out.

It wouldn't be so bad if the guy weren't on the inner thigh machine, the one all women walk right by and think *Oh, Hell no.* It's the one where you stick your feet in stirrups not at all unlike the ones attached to the gynecologist's table, but without the little heel socks that advertise the birth control drug that ensures you're only in that position once a year. Then, with your legs splayed in such a way that makes you self-conscious about the degree to which you've sweat thus far in your workout (your swamp-ass factor), you use your inner thigh muscles to close your legs like a lady while all the forces in the universe fight to keep your legs wide open. This machine (clearly invented by a pervert) deserves a first-class ticket to the same circle of hell as people who wear jeans while they work out.

I instantly want to block every vision and thought from my brain since I can't unsee this portion of the gentleman's workout. I move to the lat pull machine in an effort to be a good citizen of my own little world, but then the jeans-clad grandpa in question positions himself on the hamstring machine directly across from me so that the reinforced (thank God) Levi's 501 butt seam is directly in front of my face, where there is a faint line of butt sweat that will be burned into my retinas until my therapy sessions successfully repress it. More like Levi Swass.

From my workout bag, I pull the laminated set/rep indicator I refer to even though I know the ins and outs of this routine like my own heartbeat (77 at resting, 124 at moderate cardio, 170 at vigorous cardio) so I can stare at something besides man butt sweat. I figure the universe will forgive me if I cut my lift short, given the present circumstances. The indoor track looks far more inviting, and at least the "scenery" will rotate. I try not to think about the fact that it will also give me an opportunity to scope out something to add to the collection in Room 403, because my therapist said I needed to embrace good thoughts or something. Probably not what she meant, though.

I feel like lately every time I've been in here all I've done is gone running, which seems a little ridiculous since it's the one exercise I can do anywhere. But it makes me feel better, so fuck it. I push the thought from my head and pull the laces of my running shoes a little tighter. These shoes have way too many miles on them and I know I need to replace them, but every time I go to buy new ones I can't find any that aren't covered in the neon vomit pattern that is so inexplicably popular these days. Don't the good people at Asics know that I prefer not to stick out? When did solid black or white athletic shoes fall out of fashion, and why didn't someone have the courtesy to warn me in advance so I could stock up?

I work up a brisk jog and move into the "fast lane". As I round the first corner, a glowing shirtless gentleman comes into view in the middle lane, and the view is good. I slow down a bit to savor the image as I pass him, glad my view is not sullied by denim workout apparel. *This is more like it.*

"Good morning," he says without any hint of labored breath, which catches me off guard a bit.

"Thanks." *It's a good one now.* I debate whether to peek over my right shoulder but worry that this will be the exact moment my shoelaces magically untie themselves and I trip over my own feet and fall to my death, landing on the free-throw line of the freshly buffed basketball court below. This would be doubly unfortunate since someone down there has left his iPod Touch unguarded (not that I need another one of those). I opt to keep both eyes forward and pick up the pace so I can see the front half of the polite (and sculpted) gentleman from the other side of the track.

As luck would have it, the vinyl court partitions have been

stretched from ceiling to floor in preparation for square dancing (an activity I still have nightmares about from fourth grade), which completely obscures the view I was so desperately hoping for. He crosses the partition at the exact moment I do, on the other end of the gym. Instead I see old man Levi Swass in the middle of a triceps curl, which makes me wince.

I don't even realize I've slowed down until the "Good morning" voice is talking to my backside. I secretly hope he finds his view as pleasant as mine.

"Are you that wiped out from trying to outrun me?" he asks the ass I've worked very hard to keep hard. I turn around only to recognize the face I'd been trying in vain to see, a face that belongs to my past treadmill buddy who failed to see the journalistic merit of *Washington Journal*. I feel my face flush and I'm not sure if I tell it stop mentally or out loud (which seems to be a pattern with this gentleman).

I did outrun you. "I'm not trying to outrun you. This is my cool down," I say, hoping the sweat clinging to my hairline for dear life doesn't give me away.

"All the same, I still think we could use your speed on the court. Have you given any more thought to my offer?" he asks with a smile I'd previously neglected to notice. It's a smile that could be on a wall in one of my father's patient rooms.

I'm confused, which probably registers on my face because he backs up a couple steps, maybe wondering if he's carrying on a conversation with the same person he spoke with on the treadmill a couple days ago. Like I said, I am pretty plain looking and I like to think I blend in quite expertly. "What offer?"

He crosses his sculpted arms over his bare (and less-sculpted, though not entirely unimpressive—not that I am staring) abs. "Dodgeball? Thursdays? Forgive me if I didn't have the courage to ask you before, but I'm pretty sure I did."

For all my brainpower, I have a difficult time registering whether this guy is flirting with me or if he really is that hard up for a teammate. Who does this guy think he is, asking a complete stranger to join an inner circle without considering that I might be a complete sociopath (which, my therapist assures me, I am not; I merely have sociopathic risk factors due to my inability to form what she calls *normal* relationships)?

"Why do you want me?" I ask, hoping he doesn't take that question to imply what I realize too late could take on a whole other meaning. If he does, he doesn't show it, but shrugs ambivalently.

"You're in here all the time anyway. You're in good shape. We need a woman. You *are* a woman. Why wouldn't we want you?" I can't help but feel knocked down a peg or two, noticing his choice of pronoun—*we*, not *I*.

"You don't even know me." *And you don't want to—trust me.*

"You're right; I don't." He extends a hand that looks rough, but not too rough. Somewhere in between data entry technician and jobsite foreman. "I'm Joe."

Joe. Average Joe. Wouldn't we make quite the pair? "I'm . . ." I start to say my name but the three-letter word won't fall out of the mouth I've used more in the last two minutes than in the last two days. *Ann. Your name is Ann. Just say it.*

"You're . . .?" his hand still hangs awkwardly, waiting for me to accept it and my part in this social contract. Instead, though, I turn and run in the opposite direction, making a beeline for the stairs that lead to the women's locker room. He can't find me there.

I take the stairs far too quickly for my legs (all noodly from the weightlifting) to handle and I nearly trip over myself on the way down, but somehow stay upright. I don't even stop at the water fountain before darting into the locker room, the fluorescent-blub-framed mirror showing me exactly how red with embarrassment my face is. Thankfully, the locker room is deserted, which gives me a chance to take the five deep, cleansing breaths my therapist advises when I start to feel anxious.

I normally don't steal anything from the locker room because it's such low-hanging fruit I frankly find it almost insulting, but this is an emergency. Among the bevy of half-zipped duffel bags and belongings piled into pillars of trust on the locker room benches, I spot a pair of rainbow-colored, sequined ballerina flats that just happen to be my size glittering brightly under the corner bench.

I don't even care that the owner of these shoes also owns a dog who clearly enjoys the taste of insoles. I slip my sweaty feet into the partially-chewed flats and (after checking to see the coast is clear of Average Joe), make my way to the north exit.

"Hi, Ann!" Jeanette's wide grin says to me just as I push the bar on the door to make my hasty exit. I'm far from in the mood for small talk, but it's just so hard to be rude to someone so damned chipper and nice all the time.

"Hey, Jeanette," I say, making what I hope are imperceptible centimeter increments out the door. "I'm just on my way out."

"Wait!" she exclaims, throwing both arms out in front like she's getting ready to do the set of high knees I cut out of my routine. "Just real quick; I want you to meet Remy." She knocks on the glass window of the office behind her and a large, dark-skinned man in a uniform steps out.

"This is Remy. He's our new security guard. This is Ann. She's one of our regulars; she's in here all the time."

Remy extends a large hand and once again my brain has to force me to pick up my right arm and take it. My feet are burning in my stolen shoes and I have to look down to make sure that the security guard doesn't possess some superpower that makes stolen goods glow bright red or something.

"Ann." It's all I can manage to choke out.

"Remy. Looks like we'll be seeing a lot of each other, then. You can help me keep an eye on this place."

I force a smile that I'm sure looks forced. "Looks like it."

Chapter 7

GUNTHER THE GRUNTER

I both love and hate it when the end of February rolls around. This is the time of year when all the people who were so unbelievably keen on creating "a new you in the new year" succumb to the new season of primetime reality TV shows and opt to stay home and eat Fritos on the couch instead of going to the gym. I don't judge too harshly; Fritos are delicious.

When the Resolutionaries are in here, even though it becomes nearly impossible to find an open treadmill, I feel better about myself. Now that they're all gone, it's just me, the old people who have nothing better to do, and the beautiful people—the career gym rats. I don't identify myself as one of this latter group, because despite my frequent comings and goings to this place, when I'm around this group of people I feel like the fattest person in this little corner of the universe. These are the people who don't just work out every day to keep red velvet cupcake ass at bay; endorphins are their version of heroin. They don't need the laminated sheet of exercises they're in the gym to do, because they are already committed to memory, but they bring the sheet anyway. They're the kind who drink pre-workout and take supplements and eat protein shakes for dinner, and have no idea what the dreaded "plateau" is like because they haven't seen a fitness plateau since puberty.

Maybe I'm just extra sensitive to the beautiful people today because according to the scale, I've been the exact same weight, to the first decimal point, for the past eight weeks. Maybe it's because instead of protein shakes I eat Cheesecake Factory take-out and Fritos for dinner far more often than I should, but what's the point of working out for twelve hours a week if you can't indulge in the occasional 1200-calorie meal? Four times a week is occasional, right?

Not for these people. For them, working out is its own reward. Assholes. I don't know why the beautiful people don't appreciate that this is a mostly taxpayer-funded community center. Why they don't go join a real gym like Gold's or Lifetime Fitness to be with their own kind, their own little community of beautiful people? People like Gunther, who I see over on the pull-up bar from my vantage point on the recumbent bike, just over the top of the book I've been reading for the past four months. At the moment, Gunther's far more entertaining than the book. His name isn't really Gunther; it's short for the name I gave him the second time I encountered him here way back when—Gunther the Grunter.

What Gunther wears couldn't really be considered a shirt—the side seams begin at a point somewhere around the hips, clearly to drive home the point that he wouldn't bother to wear a shirt at all if it weren't community center policy (thank God—especially in January with all the Resolutionaries flabbing about). And sleeves? No. Fuck sleeves. Sleeves are for people whose biceps are smaller than their thighs, which of course doesn't apply to Gunther. Naturally, before being demolished with a pair of dull scissors, Gunther's shirt proudly advertises one of his many physical achievements—today's touting the 2005 Hospital Hill Run (I conquered the hill!).

Why someone with such obvious physical strength and stamina feels the need to grunt like a hung-over brontosaurus with every single rep he performs is beyond me. I'd go back to reading my book, but Gunther's loud grunting that accompanies each pull up is my version of nails on a chalkboard. If I had fillings (thanks, dentist Dad), they'd be rattling from the sound. Seriously, get over yourself, Gunther. Everyone in this gym knows that for you, doing a pull up is about as easy as taking a dump, so enough with the grunting. Come to think of it, the grunting kind of makes it sound like he's taking a big dump.

With a final grunting motion, Gunther shrugs his broad shoulders off the bar and smiles at one of the female career gym rats, a perfectly-tanned young woman in yoga pants. I bet she and Skinny Bitch are BFFs who swap recipes for kale smoothies. As Gunther picks up a fifty-pound dumbbell and starts grunting out some melodramatic bicep curls, I swallow a little of my own vomit—mint chocolate chip ice cream flavored—and opt to finish my workout at the fitness center of my apartment complex. It's a tiny, sorry excuse for a gym, but desperate times call for desperate measures.

It's been at least a month since I set foot in the apartment gym, but the amount of equipment has visibly diminished since that time. Most of the dumbbells have to be used singly as the other half of what was once a pair are mysteriously MIA. A single ratty yoga mat sits crumpled in what I distinctly remember being an orderly pile. Snapped cables hang in disrepair from weight machines under a fine layer of dust.

There's only one other person in the gym with me, a young mother whose newborn baby is napping on her chest as her legs work the recumbent bike. That's another thing—it doesn't matter when I choose to go to this gym, there's always someone using the ONE machine I planned on using. Of course, there's only one recumbent bike in here, so I settle for an elliptical machine that's more of a glider, which makes it the most useless piece of fitness equipment ever made: all the effort of running, with none of the benefits. I could run outside if it weren't February. I could run inside if I didn't feel like it was the only exercise I've done lately.

From the one TV in the upper corner of the room, the woman on the bike is watching HGTV at ear-splitting volume, which makes total sense for someone who lives in an apartment. Still, usually when I'm in here someone's watching Real Housewives of Wherever or Duck Dynasty, so it could be worse. And there's someone who always watches the Food channel. Who watches the Food channel while they're working out?

I bang out twenty more minutes so I can hit my cardio goal for the day and walk back to my apartment. After assessing the status of my fridge's contents, I call Cheesecake Factory to place my takeout order and flip on my computer to see if I have any job invitations on eLance waiting for me. I don't, so now I should go search for some and apply for them myself.

The Zeppelin cardigan I stole from the community center a month ago is draped over the chair behind me, and I slip my arms in the holes and breathe in the familiar scent once again. Next to my mouse, the iPhone I'd found in the pocket of the cardigan sits, prompting me to enter the passcode to unlock the screen. I should be applying for jobs, but instead I find myself fixated on figuring out the four-digit combination while I wait the fifteen minutes for my Diana Pasta to be ready. Whatever yummy-smelling gentleman this phone belongs . . . belonged . . . to, he's not a total idiot. His passcode isn't 1-2-3-4, 5-6-7-8, 0-0-0-0, or the numeric equivalent of BOOB. I am so entranced with solving this mystery that when a text message notification flashes on the screen, I look up and realize twenty-five minutes have already gone by. The text message is from "Tina Willis (Mother)." Not Mom. It reads: JOEY UR FATHER WANTS U 2 CALL HIM

I try tapping the text notification to see the history, but am once again prompted for the passcode. My birthday doesn't work this time either; I think I've tried that once before. I carelessly drop the phone back in its place next to the mouse, where I write "Joey Willis" on the corner of a piece of paper before I can forget. My takeout's getting cold.

Chapter 8

BURPEE BEYONCÉ

I 've added circuit training to my weekly workout rotation, if for no other reason than because I am just that much of a glutton for punishment. As I quickly discover any time I think I am in good enough shape to easily pick up a new activity without constantly getting that close-to-death feeling, I am not. The same is true of circuit training, which I am currently slogging through on a Monday night, when floor space is a precious commodity due to it being the most crowded evening of the week.

My next exercise in this circuit is burpees, which I am convinced are an actual manifestation of the devil. I quickly swallow a gulp from the rapidly depleting water bottle advertising my dad's dental practice, Josephson Smiles, and try to position myself in a spot where I won't kick anyone else in the face. As I approach the first squat position, a Beyoncé video begins playing on the community center's closed-circuit television.

I've been doing these circuits for about five weeks now, and I've gotten better at everything except burpees. I've tried them with pushups, without pushups, with jump, without jump, and every permutation thereof, and I am still unable to squeeze out more than five burpees in a thirty-second interval, and my circuit interval is two minutes, which is a full two minutes of that close-to-death feeling. It's embarrassing, really. I'm in here almost every goddamned day and I can't do a two-minute series of burpees without stopping to gasp violently for air or ending up with a vertical jump that more closely resembles a bunny hop.

I want to mentally go to my happy place as I slog through the burpees, but instead I find myself watching the Beyoncé video and getting exponentially angrier with each rep. How many years of burpees would I have to do have her perfect body? Sure, all the Cheesecake Factory takeout I eat doesn't help my cause any, but I am in this building every day and my legs would still look like a vat of cottage cheese in Beyoncé's neon green fringe dress that appears every twenty seconds in this video. I'm convinced I'll never be able to burpee my way into being Beyoncé.

Once a month, I have to meet my parents for dinner at their place of choice. It's our mutual unspoken agreement that in exchange for this meeting, at which I tell them all about the freelance jobs I am taking on, my appointments with my therapist, and some semblance of a social life, they in turn continue to pay the better part of my bills for the next thirty days. Plus, they pay for dinner, so it's not all bad.

This month, they want to go somewhere "close to home," which of course means their home and not mine. They live in Leawood, which is just as hoity-toity as it sounds. There is a mall there with stores like Williams Sonoma that normal people never set foot in. We agree on North, an overpriced "American cuisine" place in this hoity-toity mall in this hoity-toity suburb of the greater metro area that sells a twelve-dollar version of a fast-food hamburger.

My mother is already refilling an empty glass of Malbec when the hostess clad in a backless black dress escorts me to their table; my father is finishing off the last of a large plate of the fried calamari he knows I don't like.

"You're ten minutes late," my father says. "I wasn't going to say anything but your mother was worried." The fact that she was worried does not surprise me, but I have trouble believing the worry was ever directed toward me. My mother is one big machine gun of worry that shoots at indefinite targets. She worries about anything and everything as long as it has no immediate personal impact: climate change, the Affordable Care Act (I refuse to call it Obamacare), child labor in Bangladesh, the world's growing resistance to gluten, farm subsidies, genetically-modified organisms, ISIS, you name it. If she went to Dr. Andrea Kelley like she's made me do since puberty, I bet the doctor would tell her that she chooses to worry about all these distant external stimuli as a way to avoid dealing with feelings and crises about things closer to home, but I'm just speculating.

"What's good here?" I ask, burying my face in the menu that, at three feet tall and six inches wide, is an unnecessary dimensional oddity.

"Everything is good here," says my mother, sloshing wine in the hand that flourishes to make her point. I order the twelve-dollar burger that doesn't even come with fries and probably won't be any tastier than the one I got at Hardee's on Tuesday, but at least I won't get a mad cow lecture from Mom given that the menu description reads "farm-to-table ground Wagyu beef sirloin." I like my burgers on the well-done side, but I order it medium because the idea of ingesting slightly bloody pink cow is more appetizing than having more potential conversation time elapse between now and when the food arrives.

"We've been having the craziest weather lately," Dad says. I know this already because I only live ten miles away and therefore have relatively identical weather, but I smile and nod instead of pointing this out.

"We sure have."

"How is work?" Dad asks, topping off Mom's winnowing glass of wine.

"Fine," I say. "I've got about five clients lined up at the moment." I only have two, but I could have five if I wanted, so it's not really a lie.

"You're so lucky to be in technology. Everyone else out there is really struggling to find work these days. And here your kind has to actually turn people away because you've got people knocking your door down. It just ain't right," Dad says with a scowl that, rather than showing off his well-polished veneers, accentuates the deep lines on his brow. I think about saying something in defense of "my kind," but Mom pipes up and changes the subject for me. Dad excuses himself and heads in the direction of the bathroom.

"Your cousin Irene has been having seizures for the past two months. The doctors don't know what's wrong with her," my mother says. I should feel sympathy for Cousin Irene, but Irene is one of twenty cousins from my mother's side of the family I see once every ten years, so I'm having trouble just remembering which one Irene is. Besides, it's part of Mom's conversational routine. Once she's finished chronicling all the physical maladies of every person she knows, she'll move on to the obituaries of people she only knows through other people.

I keep my eyes on her but my thoughts start to wander. For some reason, the guy from the gym—the one who keeps asking me to join his dodgeball team—pops into my head. Dr. Kelley still thinks I should join the team but the thought of having to be social with all those people terrifies me. Plus, it's on Thursdays, which is Zumba's new night. Still, like he said, "You're in here all the time anyway. You're in good shape. You're a girl. We need a girl. Why not?"

Mom catches me off guard when she locks eyes on me and says, "You look happy."

"What?" I jump a little, cold-cocked out of my brief inner reverie.

"I said you look happy."

I get why this would stand out to her, as *happy* does not make the list of words people typically use to describe me. I know it's probably a mistake before I even say it, but I have no one else to say it to except my therapist.

"Mom, how do you know when a guy's actually interested in you and when he just wants something else?" It sounds as pathetic out loud as it did in my head, and pathetic is certainly a word that makes my list of descriptive adjectives.

My mother just shakes her head. "That's not appropriate dinner conversation, honey."

I roll my eyes. "I didn't mean *that*, Mother. I mean when he just wants you to, you know, be his . . . tutor. Or his spotter." I briefly consider saying "or a member of his dodgeball team" but know this will only sound like more of a euphemism, not less.

"Well, when God finds the right person for you, He will put him in your path and you'll just know," she says. I wonder how literally I should take this; does the passing lane of the gym track count as God putting a man in my path?

"Never mind."

"I certainly hope God brings you someone soon. You don't want to be providing us grandbabies at an advanced maternal age. You know sixty percent of women are having children five years later than a decade ago." She swirls her wine.

I'm about to pipe up that I am far from what any medical professional would consider advanced maternal age, but Dad returns from the bathroom. I want to see things from her point of view; when she was my age, she already had a three-year-old. Right now, though, all I can see is her resting bitch face staring down another nearly empty glass of wine. Our food arrives. The bottom bun is soggy with the bloody juiciness of the burger, and it makes my stomach turn.

"Let's pray," Dad says. They always do this at restaurants. Why couldn't they have gotten this out of the way while they were waiting for me to get here? I bow my head and look at my very sore quads. Fucking burpees. I sigh, waiting for Dad's voice to start and finish the prayer in about three seconds, without so much as taking a breath, like usual.

"BlessusOhLordandthesethygiftswhichweareabouttoreccive-fromthybountythroughChristOurLordAmen."

"Amen."

Three days later, as I am on my way to the gym for Zumba night, I stop by the mailbox at the front of my apartment complex. Lying inside is a two-CD set: *Dating & Courtship: Pacing of Intimacy for Adult Catholic Singles*. Thanks, Mom. I'll probably leave it inside someone's bag at the gym. I can't wait to tell Dr. Kelley all about how I have completely turned around my sociokleptomanical behavior. Who even owns a CD player anymore?

Chapter 9

VOODOO WOMAN

As I pass through the first set of doors at the north entrance for Zumba, it suddenly dawns on me that Zumba night is also dodgeball night. Dodgeball is played in the Mavericks gym, which sits right next to the entrance I had the misfortune of choosing. At this point I have two choices: I can continue through nonchalantly, hoping Average Joe doesn't see me, or I can hightail it around the building to the south entrance. The latter choice sounds like the better of the two, until I see Remy the new security guard step out of his office into the lobby. If I turn around now, he'll see me and wonder why I'm backing away, even though this is ironically the one moment where I'm not doing anything wrong.

Still, I'd rather not needlessly invite suspicion, for one. For two, there are countless piles of unattended belongings in the lobby courtesy of the people playing dodgeball. At the sight of this, my spine starts to tingle. It's kind of like in those old Looney Tunes cartoons where instead of seeing the Roadrunner, the

Coyote sees a perfect Christmas ham—except instead of seeing random piles of stuff, I see sparkling pirate's booty in a mahogany treasure chest.

Remy the security guard begins a slow, serious saunter to the front door I would be walking through right now if my feet were working. His face is intimidating right up until the moment he flashes a smile my dad would frame and put on the wall of his tooth extraction rooms, his teeth looking extra white against his black skin. For such a large metropolitan area, Kansas City is very racially segregated, and Johnson County is about as colorful as a ream of printer paper.

"Good evening, Miss Josephson," he says in a voice that's two parts cinnamon and one part arsenic, opening the door for me and greeting me with a bow that only makes the black-guy-in-Johnson-County stereotype worse. I'm stunned he knows my last name. No one knows my last name. Heck, if he hadn't reminded me, I wouldn't even know it now.

"Yes. Good evening," I say, averting my eyes which inevitably fall to the coat rack where an adorable knockoff Burberry pea coat that would look great on me hangs askew.

"What are we hittin' tonight?" he asks, standing too close to me. "Treadmill? Lap pool? Zumba?"

I'm here for Zumba, but I could just as easily follow my instincts and turn and run out the door instead. It's not like I absolutely need to be here tonight; I can always make up the missed workout tomorrow when I feel more combobulated. It's been far too many seconds since he asked me a question and I have yet to answer.

"Nothing, actually," I say behind the most genuine smile I can muster at the moment. "I-I . . . just forgot my coat!" The words come out of my mouth before I have a chance to evaluate the stupidity of what I just said, or what I was about to say. He looks at me like my dad would have if he'd ever known I was lying, but he's apparently not as intuitive as Remy. A familiar voice from behind both shocks and rescues me.

"She's here to fill in on our dodgeball team tonight." It's Average Joe (that was his real name, right?) and he says it so matter-of-factly that I am rendered unable to protest. He's got me in a corner. I remind myself to never say that previous sentence to my mother. I spin around to meet his sparkling eyes and matching smirk long enough to feel my face flush, then return my gaze to Remy.

"Yep," I say. "That's right. Wish me luck; it's my first time."

Without invitation, Average Joe grabs my hand and leads me to the freshly lacquered basketball court I've never actually set foot on except to quickly swipe something from one of the soccer moms doing step aerobics to Rihanna. He's spouting off the rules of the game to me and I'm trying to listen and comprehend while discreetly doing the deep breathing, anti-anxiety routine Dr. Kelley taught me, trying to counteract the panic I feel rising up in my esophagus. Again, I want to turn and run out the door, but as I look over my shoulder, I see the imposing figure of the security guard lurking just outside the double glass doors, our audience of one. I am trapped. I am hopelessly, miserably, fucking, trapped.

I spin around to see a referee donning the stereotypical striped shirt and short black shorts uniform, arranging six equidistant bright orange foam balls about the size of a soccer ball on the half court line. This isn't the dodgeball I remember from recess. Where is the giant red inflatable rubber ball with the texture capable of taking your skin off? I realize I should probably be listening more carefully to Average Joe's explanation of the rules, given I have no idea what I am doing. Then again, maybe there's still time to secure a spot as dedicated benchwarmer.

"I'm not much of a team sports kind of person," I say in a voice that comes out much meeker than I intend.

"You'll do great," Joe says, releasing my hand only long enough to place both of his on my shoulders before leading me to the sideline. "It's best three out of five. You can sit this first match out to see how it's done, but after that, we'll need you out there because we have to have two women on the court at the start of each game."

There are three women, including myself, on the sidelines, and one of them looks like broiled death with the entire sinus area of her face a bright red. She makes her way onto the court far to the left, which I quickly discover is the side of the team that does not sprint to the middle to grab one of the foam balls that are nothing at all like the ones I got pummeled with on the grade school playground. She is the first one to be whistled out, with a shot directly to the babymaker, which she barely acknowledges as she makes her way back to the sideline and collapses against the wall in a raspy fit of coughing. No wonder they were desperate enough to enlist me.

From our sideline, I hear a repeated accusation of "Two balls! Two balls!" and before I can giggle (because I am little more than a twelve-year-old boy trapped in the body of a clinically disturbed twenty-five-year-old woman), I gaze over at the opposing team to see a player drop the ball he was holding in his left hand and pretend he didn't know what our team was squawking about. The ref blows the whistle with more force and motions him off the court. I make a mental note that holding more than one ball at a time is a no-no.

My team loses the first match, but Average Joe makes a point to tell us it's still best three out of five, and to shake off the first loss.

"You," he says, pointing in my direction just outside the circle the team naturally formed without being told to, referring to me as "you" since this is, to date, the only name he knows me by. "You're in this time. Do you wanna run?"

I have no idea what he is talking about. "Yeah, okay."

A very tall, very skinny team member extends his arm to shake my hand as we make our way to the court. "Hey, I'm Mike."

I take his hand and shake it like a normal person would. "Ann."

"Nice to meet you." Out of the corner of my eye, I see that Average Joe has just witnessed this transaction and looks a little hurt that I shook this stranger's hand and told him my name when I wouldn't do the same with him, but I don't have time to reflect on that because Mike is telling me to stand in the far-right position and sprint for the ball the ref has just placed in the center of the court directly in front of me. That's what he meant by running.

"Ann!"

I lean back to see Average Joe half-shouting my name from three positions away. "You got this, Ann!" My name sounds weird coming out of his mouth—almost as weird as being called Miss Josephson.

He hollers from across the court. "As soon as you grab the ball, toss it to me."

I nod, noticing the other two runners are making similar unspoken promises with the other two team members on the left side, the non-runners.

The whistle blows and I instinctively take off as fast as I can, not taking my eye off the bright orange ball even though I can feel the steam of the devil stare coming from the eyes of the female opponent across from me. I give myself only enough time to get a grip on the ball before tossing it back to Average Joe, whose arms are already up in catching position. As soon as it hits his hands, he rears back and lets it fly low, directly into the legs of a very muscular gentleman on the opposing team, who is subsequently whistled out.

I'm so excited about my assist that I clap my hands along with the rest of the team and jump in the air, just in time to take a ball in the shoulder from devil-stare woman on the other team. My smile falls as I hear the whistle and make eye contact with the ref, who's giving me the "You're out!" thumb. I dejectedly jog off the court.

"It's okay, Ann," Joe shouts distractedly as he dodges a throw from the other team. "You can come back in when someone catches a ball. Just watch for the catch."

I fight the tears welling up in my eyes, simultaneously hating myself for letting the team down and reminding myself that I only joined this team ten minutes ago, it's just a recreational league dodgeball game, and I'm only here because they needed another uterus to fill in for Fluey Sue. Yes, that's my new name for her. No matter what her real name is, to me, she shall henceforth be known as Fluey Sue.

Tall Mike crouches as a neon-orange heater flies across the center court straight for his gut. He catches it with his entire body and an audible *thunk*, hugging it with both arms before victoriously thrusting it in the air to signal that another teammate can reenter the field of play. As the first person to be called out this game, that's me.

I sprint back out onto the court, only to nearly trip over a ball that flies and lands at my feet. Average Joe starts to argue with the ref that the ball hit the floor first before bouncing up and hitting my feet, but I figure I should probably do the honest thing for once and admit that the ball got me out fair and square, so I do, despite the fact that I legitimately would like to stay in long enough to not fuck up.

I return to the spot on the sideline I have a feeling I'll be seeing a lot of tonight, and helplessly watch as my team gets pelted
with ball after ball until Average Joe is the only one left on the
court. We crouch on the sidelines and cheer him on with claps
and "You got it, Joe" shouts over the amplified court noise. After
several impressive dodges and ducks, he makes a jumping catch
that makes his shirt rise over the waistband of his shorts to reveal
a sliver of his pale stomach. I clap and am about to let out a holler
when I feel hands on my back telling me I need to go back in.
I run out, this time watching as a ball sails straight for my head
and ducking to dodge it.

"All right, Ann. We've got this," he says with a quick pat on the
shoulder, just as a thrown ball from the opposing team brushes the
hemline of his shorts. It's enough. He's whistled out and before I
know it, I'm standing on the court by myself, surrounded by all
but one of the six orange balls, which is being pressed menacingly
by the muscly man standing just over the line of the opposite side
of the court, a male teammate on either side.

I freeze, not knowing what to do, vaguely registering my
name being yelled over and over from my teammates on the
sideline, most of whose names I don't know. They're actually
cheering for me like they know me.

"Come on, Ann! You can do it!"

I can't. Everyone is staring at me and knows my name.
They're clapping and telling me to pick up a ball, which I do
only to deflect the one coming directly at my head. I only know
the deflection is successful because I feel it reverberate up my
ball-holding arm; my eyes were squeezed shut and my head was
turned around to avoid a shot to the face.

As I hear the other ball hit the floor, the sound is replaced by
a loud countdown from ten from everyone on the court except
the ref, whose mouth is occupied by the whistle in anticipation

of my imminent out-ness. I remember somewhere in the quick litany of the rules Average Joe laid out for me that you can't hold a ball for more than ten seconds when the other team doesn't have any on their side.

As the countdown winds down to one, I throw the ball. Well, throw isn't really the word I would use. It's more of a gentle rainbow arc that lands softly in the waiting grip of my opponent's hand, easier than catching a leaf falling from a tree. The sound of the ref's whistle echoes off the walls. The game is over.

"That's okay, Ann," the team is saying to me as they call me into the huddle, the team now down two games with three to go. Average Joe, team captain, is less positive this time.

"Let's just try to win one. We don't want to hand them three victories in a row. Same starting formation as last time. Ann, just like before. As soon as you grab that ball, you toss it back to me."

I nod, looking around at my teammates, who I expect to be burning me with their eyes but instead are telling me "Good job." This alternate dodgeball universe has warped ideas of what I'd consider good, but it's still nice not to be hated.

This time, as soon as I toss the ball back to Average Joe, I hightail it to the back of the court and try to make myself useful by feeding the fallen balls to the guys on the front lines and keeping clear of any balls flying my way.

This strategy works, and we win in less than two minutes. I cheer in disbelief. Obviously, the best strategy is to strike quickly and aim low, where it's more awkward and difficult to catch the ball. I feel the weight of the two previous losses lift a bit, and sprint to the ball at the beginning of the next match with a velocity that makes my chest burn. I repeat the strategy from the game before, hugging the back wall and gently rolling the thrown balls into the field of play for my teammates. The second victory is even quicker, but Tall Mike limps to the sideline to rub his left calf.

My heart sinks, partially because I've had many a calf cramp and it's one of the worst feelings known to man, but also because now we'll be down one of our strongest players in the game-deciding match. Captain Joe (for the rest of this game, he can be Captain Joe, but afterwards, he goes right back to being Average Joe) is giving us a pep talk, assigning each of us to one opponent.

"Ann, you've got the, the . . . Voodoo woman." As fake names go, it's not a bad one, and I know my fake names. I would burst out laughing at the moniker if the situation weren't so serious. This is, after all, a possible come-from-behind victory in a recreational league dodgeball game. "Same positions as last time, but Ann, we'll need you to attack this time."

I don't want to attack. I want to keep hugging my beautiful precious back wall and keep from being the last one out again. I don't want to be the weakest link. But I also don't want to argue, since the burning determination in Captain Joe's blue-green eyes tells me this shit just got real.

At the sound of the Game 5 whistle, I sprint for the ball and toss it back to Average Joe, turning back around just in time to see the woman with the devil stare, the one Joe has dubbed "Voodoo Woman", lob a forward pass at my midsection. I dodge it somewhat awkwardly and shuffle a few steps to my left to pick up a ball, keeping my eyes up at the opposing team as I fumble around for it.

I pick it up and sweep it at the Voodoo woman's feet, watching as she jumps over it and runs around the back of the field of play before returning to my spot. I shuffle back and forth, being careful to not get hit by any other opponents, but letting my teammates attack their designated man. Or woman. I glance back at the rest of my team out of the corner of my eye. It's just me, the other female teammate (not Fluey Sue), and Average Joe. Captain Joe. Tall Mike is cheering us on from the sideline, his cramp must've calmed down, but he still can't come back in this game.

I return my eyes to the opposing team, where Voodoo Woman is holding a ball in her right hand, getting ready to throw it at me. I crouch down like Tall Mike (thank God, I've been doing all these squats; I knew they'd come in handy for something—although I'd hoped it'd be bikini butt) and shuffle to position my midsection right in line with the ball, just in time for it to hit the spot where my third boob would be, and wedge my arms up like a shrimp fork to secure it.

The Voodoo Woman's jaw drops in disbelief as she exits the court, leaving just one opponent on the opposite side of the court. I briefly glance over my shoulder to celebrate, realizing that the team is now down to, once again, myself and Captain Joc, who had been called out but, with my catch, races back on to the field as Voodoo Woman trots off.

We both keep our gaze forward, but I can tell he's watching me out of the corner of his eye. I see him jump over one flying ball, only to attempt to catch another that bounces off his hands before he can secure the catch, and is whistled out again.

Again, I'm left alone on the court, mono a mono with Muscles. I take a few tentative steps back, telling my lungs to breathe and my brain to think. I'm all that stands between us and a recreational dodgeball league victory. Muscles has two balls on his side of the court, and holds one with both hands, eliciting a loud countdown from all teammates on both sidelines. I don't pick any balls up; I just need to keep dodging until he throws them all over to my side.

He launches a fast one right for my head, which I can't move in time for it to stun me and knock my glasses off my face. I fall backward onto the court, nearly knocking the wind out of my lungs as I hit the hardwood close to my fallen glasses. I look up to catch my breath and see the thrown ball that ricocheted off my face right above me, falling back to the floor. I remember a snippet of Captain Joe's rule vomit as the blurry orb approaches my face again.

The ball's still in play until it hits another player, the floor, or the wall.

I reach up and catch the ball with one hand, digging my fingernails in as hard as I can to make sure I maintain a good grip on it. With my other hand, I reach for my glasses so I can see, not just feel, that I really caught it. A loud cheer erupts from the sidelines. Even the opposing team is shouting "Wow" in disbelief. Everyone but Fluey Sue rushes out to help me to my feet and verify that I'm not concussed. She gets a pass.

My face flushes with embarrassment from all the attention as I bend my old frames back into place and go to the end of the "good game" line, lazily brushing the opposing team's palms and acknowledging each "good game" with a nod. Most of them sound surprisingly genuine.

"You've got to come with us to JJ's to celebrate," Average Joe says. Now that the game is over, he's just Average Joe again.

I stammer. "No, I should be getting home. I've got a lot of work to do."

"One beer," he protests. "Work can wait 'til tomorrow. Come on, it'll be fun. You're our game MVP. You were the real voodoo woman out there. That was something else."

"No, no. I'm just a fill in. I'm glad I could help, but I—"

"You gonna run away from me again?" he interrupts me, flashing the smile that renders me catatonic. I pause for an awkwardly long period of time, trying to think of a better excuse than "I've got a lot of work to do."

"Even Sarah's going to come out, and she's sick as a dog." Sarah. Fluey Sue's name is Sarah.

I pause again. "*One* beer?"

"*One* beer."

"Okay. I'm in." I haven't been to a bar with other people since my junior year of college, but surely this is one of those riding a bicycle kind of things. I start to make my way toward the exit when Average Joe interrupts me again.

"Don't forget your coat!"

I look over my shoulder at the knockoff Burberry still hanging from the coat rack, then glance into the interior of Remy's office long enough to see that it is dark. Our audience of one left at the end of his shift.

"Right. I almost forgot it again. Silly me."

Chapter 10

HAIRACHE

Huddled under the warmth of my newly-acquired knockoff Burberry coat, I don't even make it to my car before the adrenaline wears off and I realize what I've just agreed to. The last time I set foot in a bar was forever ago, but I didn't even enjoy it then. And that time, I was at least wearing something a little more party friendly than sweaty gym clothes. It would be easy enough to just get in my car and drive home instead. I just met these people; it's not like I owe them anything. I could claim that I somehow got lost in the one square mile of the metro area where I live, work, work out, and otherwise spend most of my time.

Still, I can't shake the feeling that I should follow through for once, so I mentally put on my big-girl panties and follow the line of cars to a strip mall bar I've driven by every day for three years but never set foot inside. My six-year-old car's heat hasn't even had time to kick on before we pull into the angled parking spots out front, one right after another, like a scene straight out of a teenage cult movie. I can't wait to tell Dr. Kelley that I actually went to a bar with an actual group of people at my next appointment.

I'm not sure what I was expecting on the inside of JJ's, but it wasn't what I see as I walk behind my new teammates through the glass door, frosted over from the cold air outside. They pile around a wobbly table, an audible hiss emanating from the same set of rolling vinyl chairs my grandma has had in her basement for twenty years as they sit down. Apart from a solitary guy sitting on a stool with cracked upholstery playing keno on a machine at the far end of the bar, we are the only ones here. None of the many TVs on the wall broadcasting various sports-ball events are the same size or brand. The jukebox is playing a Dave Matthews Band song that is my version of nails on a chalkboard. It's all I can do to restrain myself from throwing one of the heavy upholstered chairs into it. *See?* I tell myself, *you're making good choices already.*

"I'm going to get our champion a drinky drink," Average Joe announces with a wave that signals the champion in question is me, and I am supposed to follow him.

I follow him to the middle of the bar where the young-ish bartender stands, my feet slowly crossing the threadbare carpet that covers the hard floor, my brain wondering if carpet was the best choice of floor coverings for a bar.

"Anything you want, it's yours. On me," Joe says.

I haven't ordered a drink in a bar in a very long time, so I sneak a glance at the taps and ask for the first one I can decipher. "Boulevard Wheat, please."

"Make that two. Bottles, please," he says to the bartender. "Good choice," to me. It's not, really. Boulevard Unfiltered Wheat is pretty much the Bud Light of craft beers, but it sure beats Bud Light. I briefly wonder why Joe prefers bottles to draft, but dismiss the thought. It's the kind of thing I could dwell on for hours and falsely attribute any number of personal traits to, which is not the kind of healthy social behavior typically displayed by a young lady who goes out for drinks with her recreational league dodgeball team after the big game.

The lone guy sitting on a stool a few feet away at the far end of the bar gets up to feed more dollar bills into the jukebox. Out of the corner of my eye, I can see him picking even more Dave Matthews Band b-sides. As if I needed more reasons to cut this little adventure short; this keno-playing fuckwad is forcing my hand.

"I can't stay long," I shout but realize I didn't need to. "Ants Marching" must have sounded louder in my head.

"So, it's Ann, huh?" Average Joe says, extending the short neck of his bottle to meet mine.

"Excuse me?" I barely manage to say over the noise of the clinking bottles.

"You introduced yourself to my buddy Mike over there as Ann. When I tried asking your name, you didn't ever tell me."

"Oh. Yeah," I say, then take a big swig of my sweating bottle of beer. It tastes exactly like I remember it, but I still find myself shocked by the bitter flavor and hope Joe can't see it on my face. "Sorry about that." This is the part where I am supposed to smile and extend my hand for a formal introductory shake, so I do.

"Ann. Ann Josephson." His grip is firm yet gentle at the same time and I realize that the last person whose hand I shook was the new security guard at the community center. If I weren't so shitty at this, maybe I would do it more. He smiles back. He still has a nice smile—a really, really nice smile.

"I think that's the first time I've ever seen you smile. You should do it more often. You're beautiful when you smile," he says. I'm not sure how he read my mind like that but he did.

I flush with even more awkwardness than usual. I never know how to respond to compliments, probably because growing up the only ones I got were backhanded ones from my mother. *That sweater looks lovely on you; it distracts from your knobby knees.*

"Sorry, if you don't mind my saying so, that is. I know how some girls can be weird about compliments," he says, once again reading my mind, probably seeing the consternation I was trying so hard to keep out of my face.

"Yeah, thanks." I take another swig and steal a glance over at our teammates, pouring out pints from a pitcher at the wobbly table.

"So, what do you do, Ann?" he asks, perching one butt cheek on a barstool that squeaks and leans precariously as he does so.

"Let's not," I say before I can think of something better to say. I hate these superficial grown-up conversations, as much as I hated "What's your major?" in college or "What's your favorite school subject?" before that.

He doesn't flinch. "All right. We can table that conversation for another time. Anyway, you really saved our butts out there tonight. We would have had to forfeit if you weren't there and instead we were able to get another win. Any chance we can have you for the rest of the season?"

"What's in it for me?" I have no idea what I am doing, and I have the sudden urge to go home and begin that inventory spreadsheet of things in Room 403. I keep telling myself that eventually I'll go through everything. No time like the present, right?

"Dinner. At least once, maybe twice if you play your cards right. Hopefully even more if you don't find my table manners too repulsive." He smiles again. It's still a nice smile.

We're interrupted by Mike, the only teammate whose name I remember besides Fluey Sue, who has a real name but I've already forgotten what it is. He demands that we come sit with the rest of the team with far more enthusiasm than I am comfortable with. I've made quick work of my beer since I don't know what else to do, and now it's almost empty. I protest that I need to leave.

"Oh no, dude," he says. I haven't been called dude since puberty. "We're getting some more pitchers. You can just get in on the pitchers."

It's probably not appropriate to say I don't drink beer you can buy by the gallon, and it's probably not true, either. Since I have no excuses and I've already come this far, I feel like I have no choice other than to follow Mike and Joe (who now knows my last name but I don't know his for sure) to the table.

The people are generally nice enough, but it's been so long since I had a casual conversation with anyone that I find myself shrinking further and further into myself and answering the same kinds of superficial grown-up questions I deflected with Joe as brusquely and vaguely as possible.

"So how do you know Joe?" an exotic-looking woman with curly black hair asks me.

"I don't really," I say, holding my pint glass of Bud Light with both hands as if it were hot chocolate. "We just run into each other at the gym sometimes."

"Oh, do you go there a lot?"

You might say that. More polite yet idle conversation. I cringe. "Yeah."

"I don't think I've ever seen you there before."

That's kind of the idea. Then again, I haven't seen her either, at least not often enough to come up with a code name for her. If I had, I definitely would have dubbed her Hairache because the entire time I was paying attention to her during dodgeball all I could focus on was her giant curly ponytail and wonder both how it stayed in place and whether it hurt her head. It must have, otherwise she'd still be wearing the ponytail. Personally, I pretty much live in a ponytail. It's the best way to live, hands down.

Joe sits next to me but doesn't look my way or say anything to me as his friends exchange conversation about what they're doing this week and I sit in silence, listening interestedly but feeling very much like the outsider I am. It's not their fault; they tried to engage me in conversation. I'm just really shitty at making small talk. If only the voices in my head did small talk, I'd definitely be more practiced at it, because I talk to them a lot. I can't help but notice that Joe is still sticking to his bottled beer despite everyone else pouring from the community pitchers.

I can't wait to leave, but I also don't want to be the first one to bail. So, I wait until the first person throws cash on the table before I turn to Joe, semi-privately.

"I really should go, too. I have a lot of work to catch up on." *The work that I refuse to tell you about for completely irrational reasons.* I force a smile, both hoping it will take the sting out of leaving prematurely when everyone else seems to be having so much fun, and that I'll get a smile in return. I don't. Shame—I genuinely enjoy looking at that smile.

"Workaholic, eh?" he asks.

Oh, if you only knew how wrong you are. "How much do I owe you for the pitcher?" I ignore his question, trying again with the smile, trying to appear more genuine this time.

At this, he puts a hand on my shoulder. Not an affectionate hand, more of a buddy hand. "Not a thing. It's my pleasure. You can buy the next pitcher after our next win."

I don't say anything. I almost forgot that I still haven't given him an answer about either being a permanent fixture on their dodgeball team and the dinner invitation(s). Was it an invitation? Was he asking me out or just doing the socially acceptable thing?

People don't normally ask recreational league teammates to solo evening meals, do they?

"Let me walk you to your car. The parking lot gets slippery out there," he says. I wonder if he's saying that to warn me of slipping and falling on the ice or warning me because if I do, he'll feel obligated to catch me and is afraid I'll respond with a mean left hook.

It's not that slippery out, and my car is only twenty feet away from the front door, but I let him escort me anyway. I chirp the alarm before I unlock the car.

"I didn't mean to put you on the spot like that," he says. "If you don't want to be on the team, you don't have to be. It would be nice to have you, is all. And you don't have to have dinner with me either. Unless you want to, that is."

I feel so. fucking. stupid. I can't form a logical thought to save my life, so I just come out and say the thing that I've been wondering for what feels like hours, but has probably only been a few minutes. I can still hear Dave Matthews Band, and I desperately want to get in my car and listen to something less vomit-inducing. "Are you asking me out?"

He looks confused, adequately. "Um, yes." He smiles. I really like looking at that smile. *Goodbye resolve.* "I thought I was kinda obvious."

My voice comes out barely above a whisper. "Okay. When?"

Chapter 11

GLADYSES

Tuesday open swim starts at 6:30 p.m., and arriving a fraction of a second after 6:20 p.m. typically means I'm out of luck for getting a swim lane. Because of this, I am booking it through the south doors of the community center and barely even utter a polite yet terse return "hello" to Jeanette as I punch in my access code. I only glance at the bulletin board long enough to see that the day's pool temperature is eighty-five degrees as I fly down the hallway.

My heart sinks when I enter the locker room and see that there are already some ladies from senior aquarobics brazenly disrobing. Open swim is right after the senior aquarobics class, the one I have to watch for at least ten minutes in order to get a swim lane, because the old biddies commandeer the entire lap pool for it. I had the forethought to put my practice suit on under my hoodie and sweat pants before leaving the house, partially to save time but mostly because I hate changing in the locker room when it's as full as it gets on Tuesdays between 6:15 and 6:45. I round a corner hoping to stow my things in my favorite locker, but one of the Gladyses (I call all female senior citizens Gladys) from the senior aquarobics class is standing buck naked directly in front of my locker with one meaty thigh on the bench, flossing her nether regions with a towel, her fat and loose skin jiggling with each motion.

I glue my gaze to my feet and turn around to find another locker, shrinking out of my outerwear as quickly as possible and grabbing my swim bag before shutting the locker door and attaching my combination lock to it. Of course, I use a lock; wouldn't want anyone stealing my hoodie. I'm clearly not as trusting as my fellow community center members are. I shuffle my way past two more naked Gladyses sitting on a bench without so much as a towel to act as a barrier between bench and bare ass, talking casually to one another as though their pancake boobs are not just hanging out as part of the conversation. I make a mental note to never ever use that locker room bench again. As I swing the door to the pool area open, a rush of much warmer air hits me. My strides are as long as I can make them without running (wouldn't want one of the high school–age lifeguards to blow the whistle on me) as I cross the recreational pool area to the lap pool, ignoring the high-pitched squeals of children playing under the mushroom fountain and flying down the twisty water slide.

The lap pool is separated by a wall from the leisure pool, except for one five-foot stretch of the leftmost swim lane where for some reason, instead of logically putting up a rope or a barrier, a lifeguard sometimes stands to prevent little ones from floating into someone's backstroke. There is no lifeguard posted at this spot tonight. The Gladyses who are less eager to get out and socialize naked in the locker room are still finishing class, and the lap pool is half full of elderly women and one man with a wide, creepy smile as they move through their final exercises.

I look down at the end of the lap pool, where two of the three swim lanes have been symbolically spoken for by someone else's equipment. The only lane available to me is the leftmost lane, the one adjacent to the frolicking children. The rightmost lane against the wall is my favorite, and for a brief moment I consider staking claim on one half of it, but ultimately decide that taking the worst lane for myself is still better than having to share the best one with someone else.

I drop my swim bag at the end of the lane to call dibs on it, fishing out my goggles, swim cap, ear plugs, and water bottle. Clearly, I am not as prepared as whoever will be swimming in the center lane, whose "dibs" spread is replete with a laminated list of strokes, resistance gloves, a kick board, a pull buoy, and foot fins. A couple of serious-looking swimmers sit on the bench lining the far wall, waiting to pounce on their claimed swim lanes as soon as senior aquarobics is over. One, a woman who is already sporting her goggles and a bright pink swim cap, wears an ostentatiously patterned competition suit that makes my black one-piece practice suit look boring. The other is a spray-tanned middle-aged man in a very small black Speedo sitting with his right ankle propped on his left knee, which is a very unfortunate position for someone wearing a very small black Speedo. I try not to make eye contact as I pass them and lower myself into the hot tub to wait for senior aquarobics to end.

I glide over to the side of the hot tub that doesn't have flesh-colored foam floating on top of the bubbling waters and lower myself down so that my chin touches the surface. Stretching my arms and shoulders, I let the heat of the water help my muscles along. The peppy aquarobics music stops and the instructor dismisses the Gladyses (and one old dude). The two swimmers on the bench emerge and sit on the edge of the pool, impatiently staring down the instructor as she retrieves the lane line barriers from the reel at the opposite end of the pool, resetting the lap timer as she does so. I hang out in the hot tub for a bit longer, knowing it will take a while for her to walk the colorful lane lines the length of the pool. At this point, anyway, there's no one else jockeying for position in my crappy swim lane.

When I exit the hot tub and stretch my white swim cap over my head, using the bun at the base of my neck as an anchor, I realize how much the sound of the kids playing is amplified without the aquarobics music fighting for air space. I smash the silicone ear plugs into my ears, far deeper than it says to do so on the box. I plunge myself into the warm water, admiring the way it and the ear plugs muffle the outside sounds. As I stand up and position my goggles on my face, one of the ladies from senior aquarobics waves at me. She usually stays behind to walk the length of the pool back and forth for a while after class ends, always in the rightmost lane (the one I like most). Maybe she doesn't like all the naked Gladys locker room conversation either. I don't mind sharing a swim lane with her. She keeps to herself and stays out of my way. Tonight, she's sharing the good lane with too-small Speedo guy, whom I dub Speedo Guido. I hope his spray tan doesn't wash off in the highly chlorinated water. She introduced herself to me once before but I forgot her name. Even if I remembered, she'd just be one of the Gladyses anyway. I give a small but polite wave back.

I kick off the wall and start a slow freestyle lap, letting my arms stretch in front of me, breathing to the right on every fourth stroke. My flip turns aren't great, and my first one is farther away from the wall than I like, but I push off the opposite wall with everything I've got and keep going. I do two more freestyle laps, anticipating a thirty-second rest and moving on to three back-stroke laps. On my third return trip, I see a hazy figure in a neon-colored practice suit jumping in the lane next to me as I come up for breath. She's jumped in the side next to the lane line barrier, not the side next to the opening gap to the leisure pool and the screaming kids.

I grab the wall and stand, trying not to make it too obvious that I am gasping for air. The neon-colored swimmer smiles at me.

"Is it okay if I share your lane?" she asks, as if it is permissible for me to say "No, I'd really rather have this lane to myself and make you wait until someone else is finished and also, I failed at sharing in first grade." I know she picked my lane and not the middle one because the overtrainer in the ostentatiously patterned suit is far more intimidating than me and is already doing butterfly strokes, which take up the whole swim lane, and which I cannot do. Why is it the stroke that sounds the most innocent is the hardest one? And of course, she doesn't want to share a lane with Speedo Guido and the aqua-walking Gladys. Next time, I'll be sure to wear a thong or something equally repellent.

I grumble a quick "sure," trying not to sound too disappointed. She could at least have asked me which side I wanted since I was here first instead of just taking the good side for herself. I wait until she's halfway down the lane before I launch into a back stroke lap, tracking my eyes on the ventilation ducts on the ceiling to make sure I don't go crooked or hit my shared lane partner with a sharp fingernail. Consciously, anyway.

I breathe deeply, trying to let my tension go and focus on my form, wishing I could close my eyes and shut it all out, repeating all the calming Zen shit my therapist taught me but I never practice until it's too late. I cycle through the first two laps quickly, eager for the unspoken promise of a thirty-second rest before moving on to three breast stroke laps. On the last back stroke lap, my lane buddy's breast stroke frog kick clocks me on the shoulder. I feel every muscle in my body tense even as the warm water sloshes gently around me. I get it; it happens. I've been kicked before. I've kicked people before. I still reserve the right to get annoyed by it.

I go further into the depths of my own little happy world trying to cycle through my practice as quickly as possible, three times three times three (three strokes, three laps, three times), gasping for air as I push myself harder and harder to finish quickly. I give my lane partner more space than she really needs, so as to avoid getting kicked again. At one point during a freestyle interval, I smack a kid who floated over into my space on the head. At another, during a breast stroke, I see a kid before I have the chance to run into him and politely guide him back over to the play pool, trying to avoid saying the not-child-appropriate something that would accurately reflect the frustrated thoughts running through my head. My lane partner manages not to kick me again.

I take a big gulp from my water bottle before my last interval, just three more breast stroke laps. I quietly count "twenty-five" before kicking off the wall and starting the first lap of my final segment. The friendly Gladys is still over in the right lane slowly jogging the length of the pool. On the return trip of my first lap, I spot a kid hanging out at the five-foot spot where either a barrier or a lifeguard should be. Below the water, I see him bouncing on the balls of his feet and can tell it's the same kid I had the run-in with earlier. As I come up for air, I am shocked by a wave of water that crashes into my face and goes right down my throat, open wide to take a deep inhale. I stand in the pool and cough up the water the kid splashed into my mouth before I give him a stare that probably frightens the piss out of him, given the panic-stricken look he makes in response before slowly backing away. I'd know for sure if the community center would spring for that magic stuff that turns the water dark blue when someone pees in the pool.

"Hey!" I yell at him, having reached my boiling point and not caring whose over-privileged Johnson County family this kid belongs to. "Stay away from this part of the pool. This is not a play area."

A mother comes over and stands where, again, there should really be a lifeguard. Or a rope. Or a sixty-foot wall. This is a goddamned safety issue.

"Is there a problem, Carsten?" she asks the kid, ignoring me, the swimmer in the black suit and white swim cap still coughing up chlorine and (probably) piss water.

"Yeah, there's a problem," I say, ignoring the fact that she's ignoring me. "Your kid splashed water in my face as I came up for air."

She shoots Carsten (what kind of name is Carsten?) a look, which he responds to by saying "No, I didn't!" in the voice all kids use when denying something they obviously did. It's the same voice I once used to blame my farts on the dog. It worked on my parents, so I can't fault the kid for trying. I can, however, fault him for being a little asshole. And I can fault his mother for naming him Carsten and believing he can do no wrong.

I can't take it anymore so I jump out of the water, cutting my losses and my practice short. I yank my goggles and swim cap off and stuff them into my bag as I storm across the concrete to the locker room. I look up as I storm off, seeing a row of treadmills behind a wall of steamy windows on the second floor. Average Joe is reading a magazine and walking briskly and I suddenly remember that we have a for-realsies date later this week. I don't know for sure, but I think this realization makes the temperature inside my head drop about twenty degrees. He doesn't see me. Part of me wonders if he was watching me swim but I figure he probably wouldn't recognize me behind goggles and a swim cap. I continue on to the locker room, where my temperature drops another ten degrees because the air in here feels unbelievably cold by comparison to the pool room. I cross my arms over my now rock-hard nipples.

I huddle under a shower with disappointing water pressure until the weak stream gets hot enough. I wash myself with my swimsuit on before peeling out of it and squeezing out the excess water. I toss it into my swim bag and wrap a towel tightly around my shivering body, huddling for warmth. As I twist my combination lock, I see a bag resting on the bench beside me with a swimmer's snorkel sticking out of it. Probably from the swimmer hogging the center lane, whom I dub Madame Butterfly. I yank the snorkel out of the bag and open my locker, slipping my sweat pants and hoodie on under the cover of my towel even though there's no one else in here.

I bend over to ruffle my hair with the towel one last time before gathering my things to leave. As I stand, Gladys the lane jogger is standing far too close to me than should be acceptable in a locker room. I jump in horror and a little gasp escapes. This is how bad scary movies start.

"I saw what that kid did to you. He should be ashamed of himself. That mother should be ashamed, too."

I don't say anything in response for far longer than is normal. "It's okay. Not a big deal. I can handle it." *Also thank you for not being an axe murderer.* I nod exaggeratedly for no reason whatsoever.

She points to the snorkel sitting on the bench next to me. "Does that help you practice?"

My eyes widen a little, I think. "Oh this? Yeah. I just got it. Haven't taken it for a test drive yet. Maybe next time." Technically, I'm not lying.

Chapter 12

HOSTESS BARBIE

"Ann honey, it's your mother. It's about 5:45 p.m. I just wanted to call and see how you were doing. You asked about boys the other day and I wanted to make sure you got my package in the mail. I'm praying that whatever you're going through with boys, God will give you guidance. I love you and hope you're well. Again, this is your mother, and it's 5:45 p.m."

I immediately delete Mom's voice mail, the voice mail that told me what time it was left and who it was from without my mom needing to tell me. Twice.

Joe is exactly on time to pick me up for the date that I keep insisting is not a date. "It's just dinner." He pulls up to the north entrance of the community center at exactly 6 p.m. I don't want him to know where I live, not yet, and he didn't flinch when I asked him to pick me up here instead of at home. How could it possibly be a date? He's picking me up at a taxpayer-funded location and I curled my hair in a locker room. Clearly, this is just dinner. Although if I ever do go on a *date*-date, I'll probably get ready here again. The lighting and the mirrors are way better than the ones in my apartment.

As I begin to push my way through the exit door, a deep voice from behind interrupts me.

"You look very nice this evening, Miss Josephson."

I haven't been called "Miss Josephson" since I was last invited to a wedding, which was an embarrassing amount of time ago. I turn around in confusion, because I can think of few people in this building who even know me by my *first* name, let alone my last. Remy the security guard shoots me a smile that is polite as hell but still manages to be intimidating given that it's attached to such a tall, imposing man. I swallow hard and force a smile.

"Thanks," I say, exiting hastily, not wanting to reopen an invitation to more conversation. He could just have easily said "I see you're not sweating through your yoga pants, Miss Josephson," which is my typical state within these walls. His eyes follow me suspiciously; I can feel them burning through me as I walk away into the half-dark outdoors.

Joe drives an Average Joe car—a nondescript sedan that could be a Toyota Corolla, a Honda Accord, a Hyundai Sonata, or a Dodge Stratus if I took the time to look, but I don't. He's exiting the car and making his way to the passenger's side to open the door for me but I don't let him get that far.

"Hi," I say as I quickly open the door and let myself in. "Let's go."

"You look really nice tonight," he says through the window of the closed passenger door and the eyes of yet another person who typically sees me in sweaty activewear.

So they tell me.

We sit in awkward silence for several minutes as he heads east. His car's interior is pristine—fresh smelling and not so much as an errant napkin partially wedged under a floor mat. I wonder if it's always like this, or if he spruced it up just for me.

"So, are you going to tell me what you do, or are you gonna make me guess?" he says to break the silence. I might be offended or repulsed by the question if it wasn't for the fact that he's smiling brightly at me as he says it. Oh Lord, that smile . . .

I shrug. "It's just not that interesting, and it doesn't really define who I am as a person." I realize after I say this that it sounds like a challenge of sorts, which I hadn't intended, but what's done is done.

Luckily for me, he doesn't press the issue further and instead raises his hands in surrender without breaking contact with the steering wheel. "Okay. Do you wanna know what I do for a living?"

"Not really." *Unless you're a pornographic movie magnate or contract killer or something equally concerning.* I don't know what pornographic movie magnates look like, but the picture in my head is nothing like Average Joe. He could probably pass for a contract killer though.

I continue, trying to sound as sweet as possible given what I'm about to say. "Can we just try and enjoy one another's company without forcing each other to make small talk?"

Although I'd told him to pick a place and I didn't need to know where we were going, I now know he's taking me downtown, probably because it seems like the fancy, sophisticated thing to do. Kansas City's downtown isn't the happening location it is in normal cites, and residents like us from Johnson County frequent downtown KC least of all. I can tell Joe isn't overly familiar with the area because he pays extra close attention to the exits and doesn't know which streets are one-way only. To be fair, I don't either. Why would I? I'm a Jo-Co resident. There are so few practical reasons to go downtown.

We turn down one of the one-way streets and I watch a series of foreclosed condos flash by above the empty sidewalks as I stare out the window. If my mother knew I were downtown after dark, she'd have an eyeroll-worthy heart attack. Joe could have taken me to a restaurant anywhere in the metro area, but he chose downtown so that I could see him as the cool, urbane gentleman he obviously isn't. I find it cute that he's trying. At least he appears to have opted for a restaurant that isn't in the Power and Light district; I don't own a dress short or tight enough or a pair of heels tall enough to blend in with the ratchets at that place.

Because downtown is a no-man's land, we immediately find parking on the first floor of a parking garage. This time, he intercepts me before I can open my own car door and offers a gentlemanly hand, which I take with a forced smile. As we make our way up the block, we pass a homeless man with a spotted mixed breed dog, its forlorn-looking face resting on his front paws. Both are shivering with cold despite it only being in the low fifties, but I can't judge them too harshly. I thought it was cold enough to wear my highly impractical angora mittens—a birthday gift from Mommy Dearest.

With all the tragedies that happen every year around the world, all the atrocities people commit against each other every day, all the children that go hungry, you wouldn't think I would feel bad for a dog with a homeless man, but I do. I should feel bad for the man, too, but instead I do what all normal suburbanites do and pretend he isn't there, asking me for change I don't have in my impossibly small designer handbag—the one I'm using for the first time since I got it for Christmas three years ago. Joe is still holding my hand, and his grip tightens as we pass the skinny mutt and his human companion.

Joe clears his throat. "Sorry, brother, I don't have any cash on me."

I see the lights of Ted's Montana Grill as we round the corner. I know why Joe chose this place; it's a safe, non-offensive, non-exotic option with broad appeal and a familiar menu. It's a chain, but not enough of a chain to make it an overtly lame choice, like Red Lobster or Outback Steakhouse. As someone who holds a VIP spot in the Cheesecake Factory rewards program, I acknowledge that I have no room to talk.

The restaurant is surprisingly crowded and I can't help but feel a bit claustrophobic as we enter. Joe clears a path through the crowd for me to follow him to the hostess stand, where he tells a leggy blonde that we have a reservation. We follow her to the far corner of the back dining room, where it's still crowded and loud, but less so, to enough of a degree that I can feel myself relax a little.

To what would be the further horror of my mother, I order a beer and hot wings, which is probably the worst first-date food imaginable, but this isn't a date. It's just dinner. Maybe if I say that often enough and pick up my beer enough times with both heels of my buffalo-sauce-covered hands, I'll believe it. I also believe that it won't take them long to whip up a plate of wings, and hope Joe doesn't ruin my plan by ordering a ribeye well done. To my relief, he doesn't question the need for appetizers and goes straight to ordering a medium-rare bison burger—side salad instead of fries.

Once our waiter disappears with our order, Joe pretends to watch the TV mounted in the corner above my head. Obviously, he wants me to be the one to initiate conversation since his normal standby topics are off limits, but I'm not going to give him the satisfaction. Eventually, the silence becomes awkward again. I am used to feeling awkward, but am surprised when I find myself wanting to make small talk because I don't know what else to say. I'm not usually confronted with situations where there is this level of pressure to say something; no wonder people rely so heavily on small talk for conversation and on their cell phones to avoid it.

I excuse myself to the ladies' room, mostly to kill more time but also to come up with something to talk about. And pre-peeing is always a good idea when beer is involved. The bathroom décor is dark and the lighting is dim, so I can barely see the sensor of the no-touch sink as I wash my hands. When the sink doesn't respond, I frantically wave my hands and mutter a frustrated "I'm a person, god dammit!" just as the blonde hostess walks through the door and stops dead in her tracks. She gives me a look a crazy person deserves to get before crossing the room, at which point the sink finally acknowledges my humanity.

"Watch the soap. It shoots out kind of fast," she warns me, a split second too late. I've no sooner leaned over and thrust my hand at the hands-free dispenser than bright pink gel squirts out and lands squarely on my left boob. I stare at the damage in horror before quickly grabbing a stack of rough paper towels from the decorative bin near the sink. I wet half the stack with one hand (thankfully the sink cooperates this time) and wipe my boob with the other. The dry paper towels take care of the excess drippy soap but shred against the knit of my sweater. I dab at the spot with the wet paper towels, which only manages to turn the shredded paper towel bits into spit wads that cling to the wool and spread a dark wet spot across my shirt. Last I heard, the lactating look was not all the rage these days.

I glance around the bathroom. No hand dryer in sight. I wince at myself in the mirror and hear the hostess peeing.

"Thanks for the tip," I say in a voice as free of sarcasm as I can possibly manage. "Is there an air hand dryer anywhere in the restaurant?"

"Umm . . . there's like, one in the employee bathroom."

"There's an employee bathroom?"

"Listen, I don't use it because the cooks always go in there to smoke and it's disgusting," she says defensively.

Facing the choices of wet boob or stale Marlboro stench, I pick out all the little wet bits of paper towel clinging to my sweater and press a fresh stack against the wet spot with as much pressure as I can, hoping to soak up the soapiest water possible before going back out to face Joe. Naturally, another restaurant patron chooses this moment to enter the bathroom. I squeeze my eyes shut. *Please don't ask.* I remove the paper towel compress and open my eyes. I'm surprised to see it doesn't look that bad. As long as he isn't staring at my chest, he probably won't notice. Guys aren't that observant, right? Except maybe when looking at a woman's chest . . .

I fold my arms across my chest as I exit the bathroom. It feels awkward crossing my arms this high so it probably looks awkward, too, but Joe's used to me looking awkward. Or he ought to be by now.

"Everything okay?" he says as I sit down on my side of the booth without moving my arms. I hunch down so my boobs are below the table, which I realize too late makes me look like I am leaning forward with something immensely intent to say. In all the boob-drying hubbub, I didn't think to come up with a topic of conversation.

Before I can think of anything semi-intelligent to say, our waiter rescues me by showing up with our food. To my delight, Joe lets his question go unanswered as I dunk the first hot wing in a vat of blue cheese dressing, after he courteously asks our waiter for an extra vat of blue cheese and extra napkins for me.

"I know I always need both of them," he says, blushing visibly, obviously worried he's just crossed over into too-presumptuous territory. "I figured I'd save the waiter a trip."

The napkins look far more absorbent than the bathroom's paper towels. Why couldn't they stock those in the ladies' room instead?

"No," I insist. "I appreciate it."

From there, we actually talk about real things: where we grew up, what stupid clubs we were in in high school, which brands of dish soap we like. (I don't mention that the hand soap in the bathroom is at the bottom of my list.) Surprisingly, I feel far more at ease than I thought I would going into this situation. He's pretty easy to talk to. He tells me he has four brothers and I tell him I am an only child—a spoiled only child with a mother in Junior League and a dentist father but no trust fund.

"Damn," he says, swallowing a bite of his bison burger. "And here I was after you for your money. Turns out I'm barking up the wrong tree." I'm grateful he ordered something only nominally less first-date inappropriate and messy as I did.

I deliberately save room for dessert, as I always do. What's the point of spending all this time in the gym if I don't get to enjoy full throttle beer and tiramisu? I blame my sweet tooth on my mother (although she prefers to get her sugar through dessert wine) and on the fact that I ate nothing but vending machine candy for lunch my junior year of high school. Do you have any idea how hard it is to indulge a sweet tooth when your father is a dentist?

"So, what did you go to school for?" he asks, finishing off his beer.

"So I could contribute to society and not be a complete degenerate. Because it's what you're supposed to do," I say, waving in the direction of our server. He indulges me with a laugh, which of course reveals his winning smile.

"You know what I mean," he says. "What did you study?"

"Small boat operations and sales," I lie. "It didn't work out."

The server rescues me from what is progressing toward so-what-do-you-do conversation.

"Did we save room for dessert or should I just leave the check?" he says, already pulling the black book from his apron, covered in food stains.

"No," I say, putting my hand up to stop his instinctive motion. I don't blame him; after all, who orders dessert at a restaurant where the dinner portions are so huge? "We saved room for dessert. Can I see the dessert menu, please?"

The server leaves to go hunt down a dessert menu that has probably been gathering dust for a while. Joe is giving me a puzzled look.

"What?" I ask.

"Nothing," he says, defensively. "It's just—I never see people order dessert anymore." There he goes, reading my mind again.

The server comes back with the dessert menu, which I scan for all of five seconds before declaring "I'll have the apple dumpling and he'll have the molten chocolate cake."

"No, no dessert for me, thanks," he says. "I will take a bowl of potato soup to go though, please."

"He'll have the chocolate cake," I say to the server. To him, "You know it's rude to let a woman eat dessert all on her own."

He rubs his belly. "Can't you see I'm watching my girlish figure here?"

I give him a blank look. I'm not good at this sort of thing so I don't know whether I'm supposed to pout playfully or politely decline dessert altogether or what. Just when I was starting to feel comfortable, I now feel the need to start squirming in my seat and estimating the number of steps between me and the nearest emergency exit, which I of course immediately identified as soon as we sat down.

"Okay fine," he relents. "I'll take the cake. No whipped cream, though." As if the absence of whipped cream calories somehow negates the pint of semi-liquid chocolate.

The server drops off the Styrofoam bowl of soup, the check, and our desserts. He only eats two bites of his, but it's enough to make me feel less guilty about inhaling my own.

"Do you want to take the rest of this home with you?" he asks.

"Oh no you don't," I say. "You're going to eat the cake if it takes you five days to do it."

"Don't think I won't," he says, discreetly palming the check and handing his credit card to the server.

On our way out, he grabs the individually wrapped plasticware sitting in a Longaberger basket by the hostess stand. The same hostess is standing there, smiling smugly and eyeballing my now-dry boob. *Fuck off, Hostess Barbie.* He holds my coat as I awkwardly slip my arms into it and opens the door for me as we leave, like I imagine a picture-perfect gentleman would be on a first date. Or just dinner.

"So, will you let me buy you beer, hot wings, and apple pie again some time?" he asks as we step into the empty frigid downtown sidewalk. It's gotten colder since we first got here. I slip on my angora mittens.

"Why do you like me?" I say before I can think of saying something less shitty.

He doesn't seem fazed by my unfiltered outburst—a bit confused, maybe, but he doesn't even slow his stride as he analyzes my face for clues as to what to say. Finally, he grabs my mitten-covered hand and with a smile says, "Hold that thought. Stay right here."

He releases my hand and walks up the marble steps of the Something Bank tower to where the homeless man and dog we passed on our way to the restaurant lie huddled in a dark corner.

I watch him as he hands over the bright yellow doggie bag that holds the bowl of still-hot potato soup he got from the restaurant. I can just barely make out their exchange.

"Hey," Joe says, poking the man awake. "Stay warm tonight, okay?"

"Oh! Praise Jesus! Thank you, Lord!" the vagrant says. I'd roll my eyes even harder if I weren't standing here shivering in my Steve Madden boots. *God didn't get you the soup, dude. This generous weirdo with the million-dollar smile did.*

I swallow hard and wonder if Joe's gesture is representative of his everyday generosity or if he's just trying to impress me. If it's the latter, I must admit it's working. I slowly make my way up the steps despite Joe's order to stay on the sidewalk.

"May I pet your dog?" I ask. The homeless man nods between voracious spoonfuls of soup, as though it might disappear or turn to ice if he doesn't eat it within seconds. If my mother spoke to homeless people, she'd tell him the same thing she tells me when I eat my food too quickly for her liking: "You'll feel fuller if you eat and chew slowly." I remove one of my mittens to feel the protruding ribs of the shivering mutt, who licks the warm crook of my elbow in response. *Sorry I can't lick you back, buddy. Even I'm not that crazy.*

"Here," I say, handing the mitten to the homeless man. He takes it with a quiet "Thank you." Unlike hot potato soup, I guess my mittens don't come from On High. Joe smiles at me and I begrudgingly remove the other mitten and fork it over.

Joe grabs my now-cold hand and stands me up. To the homeless man, he says "If you need a shelter, call the number on this card." I can't see what's on the card as he passes it off, but I admit it makes me instantly curious. We begin walking back toward the car.

"That dog is grossly underweight. It should be in a shelter," I say through chattering teeth.

"They should both be in a shelter," he says, releasing my hand so I can slip it into the pocket of my coat.

"Do you work with the homeless or something?" I ask.

"More often than I'd like," he says. "But we're not talking about our professional lives, remember?"

He's got me there. As we reach the car, he once again opens the door for me before I can stop him. He cranks the heater as soon as he starts the car, and I huddle into the vents even though they're just spewing cold air at this point.

"Here, I've got an extra pair of gloves back here." He reaches into the pocket behind his seat and hands me a simple pair of black gloves.

"Are you sure?"

"Of course. It's freezing out. You didn't have to give that guy your pretty pink mittens, you know. They looked much better on you." *Now you tell me.*

I slip the borrowed gloves on and breathe into my hands in a futile attempt to try and warm them quicker. As I do, I detect a scent that is moderately manly and vaguely familiar. I sniff again, trying to pinpoint the smell without making it obvious that I am some psycho smelling his gloves. Citrus. Sandalwood. My eyes go wide and I have to make sure I don't say the scent name I made up when I first stole that stupid green cardigan out loud. Zeppelin. If this were a movie, the opening riffs of "When the Levee Breaks" would emanate from the back seat right now.

"To give you a much-delayed answer your question," he says, looking over his shoulder as he backs out of the parking spot, "I like you because you're inexplicably different from anyone I've ever met."

"Most people would call that 'weird'," I say through the gloves. It's all I can think of in my brain haze.

"I prefer 'inexplicably different'," he says with his winning smile. "So, I answered your question. Are you going to answer mine, Ann Josephson?"

I'm in more of a mood to jump out of the moving car than to answer questions, but that could lead to some broken teeth, which would make my father grossly disappointed. Did I tell him my last name? When did I tell him my last name? "What question?"

"Are you going to allow me to take you out again? I'll even let you foist dessert on me."

I pause for a moment, knowing I need to end this now before things get even more fucked up than they just got thirty seconds ago. At the same time, I need him to not know how fucked up things just got. Far too many seconds have passed since he asked his question.

"Okay." It's a weak acceptance of his proposal, I know, but it's the best I could come up with.

"Are you going to let me pick you up at your place of residence this time? Instead of the gym."

"My 'place of residence'? What kind of term is that?"

"Come on now, don't change the subject."

"Maybe." My single-word answer creates an awkward stopping point for the conversation. We pull into the parking lot of the community center. It's 8:45, fifteen minutes to closing. Not even enough time to squeeze in a lightning workout, which I could really use to ease my shredded nerves at the moment. He exits the car and, predictably enough, opens the door for me before I can unfreeze my body. *Why did it have to be you?*

I step out, not sure what to do next. He must sense my anxiety, because he speaks up first.

"Are you going to give me your number so we can arrange our next meeting, or do you want to hammer out the details over dodgeball?" he asks.

The last person I gave my phone number to was my eye doctor's receptionist. "Okay."

"Okay you'll give me your number?"

"Yes." I rattle off the digits nervously before he's even pulled out his phone—his predictably brand-new phone.

"Hold on," he says. "I just lost my old phone; still figuring this thing out."

I swallow an imaginary meatball of guilt whole. After several freezing seconds, he tells me to go ahead and again I quickly dictate the digits.

"Great," he says, smiling at me. My guess is that this is the point in the evening where he's supposed to kiss me good night, but I'm pretty sure my lips are frozen together. Also, I have buffalo wing breath. Why the hell did I order those buffalo wings? He moves in for the kiss and I close my eyes. It unexpectedly lands on my cheek instead, which is probably for the best. I breathe a sigh of relief that I hope isn't audible, and smell it again as the crook of his neck slowly moves away. Citrus and sandalwood and vetiver—whatever that is—Zeppelin and perfect fucking gentleman and Average Joe.

"Be careful going home," he says with his perfect smile. "It's pretty slippery out there."

"Okay."

"Good night. See you at dodgeball."

"Good night."

I rush inside, immediately feeling a wave of artificial heat wash over me. I make my way to the locker room where I stowed my gym bag without punching in my access code because no one's at the front desk. Before I retrieve it from my locker, I sit down on the bench and move through my deep breathing exercises. I don't know whether Dr. Kelley would be proud of me for going through with the evening and putting my vulnerable self out there or if she'd be disappointed in my spazoid behavior. I feel like I ate a half pound of bacon before doing a four-mile run. The pit in my stomach feels like a lead weight, or maybe it's just the buffalo wings. I feel the guilty tears on my cheeks before I realize I am crying. I'm such a piece of shit.

I notice a strand of pearls sitting atop a neatly folded pile of clothes on the bench across from me. I wonder if they're real; what kind of idiot would leave real pearls sitting on top of everything out in the open like this? I look around. Even with there being mere minutes until the gym closes, I am in here by myself. If the pearls are real, this is the kind of thing someone would get really pissed about being gone. I close my eyes and again return to my deep breathing. I have no use for a pearl necklace. When would I ever wear it? I visualize the hypothetical moment in time when its wearer received the necklace, gifted from a loved one of course. Who buys themselves pearl jewelry? It's got to be a great memory, however it happened, and something that must mean a lot to whoever owns it.

I stuff the strand of pearls in the side pocket of my gym bag and scurry out of the gym, quickly shuffling past the front desk that is still manned by no one. If I were wearing my heart rate monitor, it would read squarely in the green zone. It would also definitely clash with my not-a-date outfit.

Chapter 13

PENNY PINTEREST

I t takes me hearing myself repeating "What did I do?" aloud to realize I am doing it. I'm sitting at home at my desk in front of my computer, where I should be getting some work done, but instead I've just spent the better part of an hour staring at the stolen strand of pearls. In my head, I've made up this elaborate story where I received the necklace as a graduation gift from my high school sweetheart, which meant I had to wait a few months to break up with him. We both knew it wasn't going to work out; I was going to one college and he was going to another. I thought I would end it easily and amicably at graduation, but since he gave me such a pretty necklace as a gift, I had to go off to college with a high school boyfriend and wait for us to inevitably grow apart, which we did six months later, but I never ended up returning the necklace. Granted, the chances that I will ever have to tell this made-up story to anyone are as minimal as the chances they would believe it, but I am prepared just in case.

Every now and then, I do have a moment of clarity. Sitting

here in my dining-room-slash-living-room-slash office, huddled in Average Joe's Zeppelin-scented cardigan, staring down his stolen iPhone and a stolen pearl necklace with a made-up story, I have one of those moments. I'm a sick piece of shit and I need help. I need to get better. I want to get better. I call Dr. Kelley's after-hours number with my own iPhone and ask to move our standing appointment up to her next available opening. She asks me if everything is okay and I lie, citing scheduling conflicts, because I am a liar. I'm sure she sees right through this, knowing the extent of my social life, but if she does, she doesn't say anything. She pencils me in for tomorrow afternoon.

Before I started making up the story of the love pearls, I again tried to crack the access code to the iPhone—Joe's iPhone. I tried his name (realizing that I never even thought to confirm his last name because I am a thoughtless shit who thinks only of herself), his brothers' names, and any other names I could pull out of the air from our lovely dinner conversation. None of them worked.

I have to return the necklace. I can't return the phone—not yet; I'm in too deep at this point. I have to come up with an exit strategy. But the love pearls? My imaginary gift from my imaginary high school sweetheart at my imaginary graduation party? I've got to get rid of these; they're nothing but trouble. I shrug off Joe's cardigan and trade it for a nondescript track jacket, shoving the necklace into one of the zippered pockets. I snatch up my keys and gym bag and head for the door.

ATTENTION MEMBERS:
THERE IS A **THIEF** HERE!
YOUR BELONGINGS ARE **NOT** SAFE!
REPORT ALL SUSPICIOUS ACTIVITY
IMMEDIATELY!

This is the sign plastered on the locker doors that greets me as I enter the women's locker room. The fact that it's printed on hot-pink construction paper in Comic Sans diminishes its effect somewhat, but the essence of the message stares me in the face nice and clear. The strand of love pearls rattle inaudibly in the zipped pocket of my track jacket. I must have pissed someone off.

The sign's working; there are no mindlessly left items sitting out in the open today. Once again, "What did I do?" is playing on repeat in my mind, but this time I am able to keep it in my subconscious, behind my big stupid mouth.

Upstairs—in the cardio room, the weight room, the stretching area, and on the track—everything looks normal. Group classes are beginning and ending like any other day. I recognize familiar faces. The adrenaline rush that surged upon seeing the pink public service announcements begins to slow to a weak trickle.

I make my way to the cardio room. It's a recumbent bike day for recovery's sake. I woke up feeling unusually sore this morning. I must have worked out harder than I thought I did before Joe came to pick me up for our date. I've accepted that it was a real date, not just dinner between dodgeball teammates, even if it did end with just a polite kiss on the cheek. Technically, I did go home wearing an article of his clothing. I now have an Average Joe outerwear starter collection.

Next to me on a stair stepper machine—the one piece of equipment I refuse to use and affectionately refer to as the tardscalator—is a woman going out of her way to look good. She's wearing tight blue workout pants from Victoria's Secret. I know they're from Victoria's Secret because they say PINK in fuchsia-colored rhinestones across the span of her posterior, which is noticeable enough just by virtue of using the tardscalator. Her coordinating pink top is something straight out of a Pinterest board, tied strips of a once-ill-fitting t-shirt down the length of her spine like a stegosaurus. It's definitely not ill-fitting anymore, and I can see the red straps of her lacy pushup bra cutting into her shoulder blades thanks to the racerback silhouette of the top.

Her chestnut brown hair is pulled back into a perfect high ponytail that swirls into a single curlicue at the end and barely moves thanks to a copious coat of hair spray, even as she climbs the fake stairs. What really kills me is her face. It's covered in a thick, fresh coat of makeup, like 8 a.m., before-work makeup . . . dinner-date-with-a-dodgeball-teammate makeup. From my recumbent bike seat that squeaks with every movement, I can practically see the bright red lipstick drying, the fresh powder absorbing the sweat. She won't shine for hours.

Even her reading material is ostentatious. Propped up on the reading ledge of the machine is a closed copy of *Pride and Prejudice* with a bookmark sticking out at the halfway point and the latest issue of *Esquire*, which she is thumbing through between stolen glances to see if anyone is noticing and/or admiring her. She might as well wear a sandwich board that reads "Please come talk to me. I am single and attractive and fit and modern and well read. Also, I have a Victoria's Secret credit card."

In my head, I think this is how some guys see every girl at the gym, when an honest-to-goodness ninety-eight percent of us are just trying to be invisible for an hour and get a damn workout in. Who in their right mind puts on makeup just to work out and sweat it off? More importantly, who works out in a pushup bra? For a brief moment, I think maybe I'm not as crazy as I thought I was this morning, but then I feel the love pearls in my track jacket pocket and dismiss that thought. I turn my tiny bike TV screen to C-SPAN. Nothing says "I am a riveting conversationalist; please come interrupt my workout and flirt with me" like C-SPAN—unless you're Average Joe and will politely strike up a conversation with any functioning sociopath, as it turns out.

I must be staring because the dolled-up woman on the tard-scalator turns to me and says a half-polite, half-annoyed "Can I help you?" Or maybe she's just finely tuned her internal radar to sense onlookers' attention.

"No, sorry," I say, clearing my throat and patting my jacket pocket from the outside to check that the pearls haven't fallen out. "I was just admiring your shirt. Did you see that on Pinterest?"

She smiles and nods enthusiastically, her perfect ponytail just barely bouncing. She must use a really good hairspray. "Yep!"

Called it. "Well, you nailed it." I return to my own little hemisphere, trying to suss out a plan for returning the necklace. Obviously, I can't just walk up to Remy the security guard and hand it over, claiming that I found it in the ladies' showers. This is going to take some clever maneuvering. The Lost and Found is a wrapping paper-covered box behind the front desk at the north entrance; you need a worker to get in there and I know they keep a half-assed log of what gets turned in and picked up. I say half-assed because not all the city government workers who are employed by the Percival O'Shaughnessy Community Center approach their jobs with equal levels of gusto; some will just mutter a "thanks" and toss the retrieved object over their shoulder into the box.

Lazy Sherrie is one such city employee. Her moniker is apt; she won't even post the day's group class schedule unless someone complains about it, and then she'll act like she's lifting bags of concrete the entire time she's stapling the paper to the bulletin board. I can't really say anything. Every time I have to redesign a logo for someone who "just wants it bigger," it feels like they're forcibly extracting a piece of my soul from my body. I would be a model municipal government employee.

Tonight is Sherrie's shift, from 3 p.m. to closing time, which is at nine. I specifically picked the six o'clock hour to come to the gym because it's the busiest. Some lesser functioning sociopaths might try to pull this off in the middle of the day when there's no one around, but if experience as a kleptomaniac has taught me anything, it's that it's much easier to hide in a crowd. The more crowded the gym is, the more distracted the staffers are, checking kids into the nursery, recovering lost access codes, showing brides-to-be the reasonably priced multipurpose room packages.

I put in forty minutes on the recumbent bike, which would typically feel like an eternity but in my evil plot scheming goes by like no time at all. I see that Penny Pinterest has moved on from the tardscalator, but I give her abandoned machine a wipe-down after I vigorously scrub my own, dabbing away at a fallen speck of glitter. I hope she found either her soul mate or the courage to try again tomorrow. I make my way down the stairs, relying on the handrail more than I'd like, but my legs are weak from the combination of yesterday's vigorous workout and the repetitive motion of the recumbent bike. I pass a middle-aged man on the stairs wearing a t-shirt that reads "F THIS." At least he's honest.

I nonchalantly retrieve my stuff from the locker room, trying my best to ignore the Comic Sans PSAs, some of which have already been torn off the lockers. I'm glad to see I am not the only one who finds them obnoxious and unnecessary, but I'm also biased. I plop down on a sofa in the member lounge where I have a good view of Sherrie's post at the front desk and pretend to watch SportsCenter on the mounted flat screen TV. As Remy the security guard walks down the hall and enters my field of vision, I snap my head forward, doubling down on my ESPN engrossment.

Out of the corner of my eye, I watch as Remy and Lazy Sherrie make idle conversation, Remy's tall frame leaning on the desk. Entering community center members give him sideways glances as they punch in their access codes, reminded that there are people of color in this universe even though they rarely see them at Pier 1 Imports. An old man pours a cup of burnt coffee from the member lounge coffee bar and changes the channel from ESPN to the local news. Weatherwoman Katie Horner takes the screen, fresh makeup remarkably similar to Penny Pinterest, glittery eyeshadow and all.

Finally, a soccer mom carrying one child and holding the hand of another makes her way in. *Jackpot.* Lazy Sherrie waits until the woman's head is down punching in her access code to roll her eyes knowingly at Remy, who gives her a half-hearted salute as if to say, "I'll get out of your hair now."

"The nursery's open 'til eight, right?" I hear the woman ask Lazy Sherrie in a frazzled voice. "Can you show me where it is?"

"I guess," Sherrie says in her fakest friendly voice, making her way out from behind the desk with an exasperated sigh.

I gather my things slowly, making sure neither Remy nor Lazy Sherrie are watching or are within my line of sight. As I walk toward the desk, I unzip the pocket of my track jacket where the love pearls have been lying in wait. Bolstered by fake confidence, I walk behind the desk and drop the pearls in.

"Excuse me," the voice from behind would make me jump out of my skin if my legs weren't so sore. A high school aged boy stands behind the desk—behind from my current perspective anyway. How dare he not bathe himself in Axe body spray to alert me of his presence like all the other boys his age?

My eyes are probably huge but I play it off. "Yes?"

"I forgot my code."

"Oh," I say breezily. "Sorry, I'm still in training and can't access the codes. You'll have to wait for Sherrie. She'll be right back."

Chapter 14

AFFIRMATION ANNIE

Dr. Kelley isn't the only one who's taken aback when I recount the events of the past week to her. Saying it out loud makes me realize how much atypical behavior has happened in such a short time. I've joined a dodgeball team (sort of), gone on a date (sort of), and returned goods that I've stolen. Sort of. On paper, I might even pass for a mostly-normal person if it weren't for the fact that I spent every hour since I woke up this morning feeling like I might rip my hair out waiting for this appointment. I also haven't yet explained what it was I stole in the first place.

"What did you take?" Dr. Kelley asks. They teach them well at—I glance at the gilded framed diploma on the wall—Northwestern. I stall, trying to think of how to explain it. I don't want to lie, but the truth sounds so horrible.

"It was a semi-valuable piece of jewelry," I say, averting her eyes.

"Semi-valuable? So not a wedding ring then?"

What kind of sociopath do you think I am? "No, of course not." I pause. "A strand of pearls."

"I see," she says, either furiously scribbling notes or doodling a masterpiece of tiny boxes. "So why did you return it? Why do you care if its owner has it or not?"

"I don't know. I guess I just felt like I should."

"Why?"

"Because it belongs to someone. Because it's not mine."

She sets her legal pad on the desk and leans forward to meet my gaze. "You're relating to people on an interpersonal level now. The team? The date? You no longer have to steal people's things to have a connection with them."

I shrug, absorbing her words about as well as an umbrella absorbs rain. "I guess you're right."

"I think," she says with a dramatic pause before continuing, "that if you keep developing these relationships with your new friends from the gym, you'll feel less and less need to indulge your kleptomania."

Never mind the fact that I indulged my kleptomania specifically because I was sent over the edge by said relationship developments. I feel like I should tell her about stealing Joe's iPhone before I knew it was Joe's iPhone, but I decide to wait and see if the topic comes up organically.

"But what if all this interaction takes me so far outside my comfort zone I snap and just make everything worse than it already is?" I ask, trying to avoid intimating that this may or may not have already happened.

"That's a fair question, and a definite possibility," Dr. Kelley says, running her fingers through her perfectly styled hair. "But you can start slow. What does a typical week of workouts look like to you? Do you count dodgeball as a workout?"

I nod. "Dodgeball one day. Ten miles of running throughout

the week. One day of swimming. One to two days of circuit training. One day of weights. One day of recovery-type cardio— elliptical or bike."

"And only one of these activities involve other people."

That's true. Group activities—never been my thing. I nod in response.

"Are there any group classes at the gym you could join? For instance, I go to a spin class on Wednesdays. It's me working toward my own personal goals, but I've got other people around me with their own goals that keep me motivated."

Spin class. No wonder her ass looks so perky in those pencil skirts. There are more group classes offered at the community center than I can count. I'm pretty sure I could go to a new group class every day of the month and not repeat a single class.

"I suppose so," I say. "Zumba—I have done Zumba before. But that's dodgeball night now."

"Okay. Start there. Shop around. Try out a few until you find something you like. I think you'll find that you actually enjoy being in the company of others despite your . . . tendencies."

That, or I'll finally snap and they'll have me thrown in a padded room. "Okay."

"Let me know how it goes," she says, almost as if she's lean- ing on me for a recommendation of what class will get her the best results in the least amount of time.

"I will."

"Close your eyes for me," Dr. Kelley says. I thought she was wrapping up our appointment, but no; she's going to have me do a visualization, an affirmation, or both. I hate doing these, but I'm not the one footing the bill for these sessions so I can't really protest. I close my eyes. She continues.

"I want you to visualize an item in your room of stolen stuff," she says. I've never told her the code name is Room 403.

"I want you to focus on an item that represents a window into the personal life of the person you stole it from," she continues. My mind immediately goes to Joe's iPhone, but technically that's not in the room of stolen stuff; it's on my tiny desk. My mind sweeps over the mental picture of Room 403. I swallow the lump of shame in my throat. I don't want to see this room. I want to keep the door to my mind as closed as I keep the door to Room 403 in real life. Near the top of one of the piles, I see the day planner I stole from Jeanette. I fixate on the day planner, complying with Dr. Kelley's instructions, almost to the point that I forget where I am until I hear her voice continue.

"Is this thing something you should have, or is it something you should return because it has some personal value that can't be duplicated by a replacement item?" I know the answer. Dr. Kelley knows it too. She's a big fan of rhetorical questions. Rhetoric must be huge at Northwestern.

"Think about how you can make amends for stealing this item by returning it, in person if at all possible," her 'visualization voice' drones on. Her last words ring in my head like church bells, or at least what I remember church bells sounding like. *In person, if at all possible.* Is she nuts (apart from the requisite amount of psychosis I imagine must be necessary for her chosen profession)? In person? How can I possibly pull that off? She begins talking again before I can let the anxiety seep into my pores and make my hands shake.

"Now let's develop an affirmation for the week. Repeat after me."

Ugh. I hate affirmations almost as much as I hate visualizations. I never feel sincere repeating the words; it's like small talk of talk therapy. Still, I let her go on and don't complain. Like I said, both her time and mine are being paid for; thanks, Mom and Dad. Just call me Affirmation Annie—accessories sold separately.

"I don't need things . . ."

"I don't need things," I repeat in my most convincing way possible.

"To connect with people."

"To connect with people."

"One more time," she says. "I don't need things to connect with people." I chime in a couple words late and say it with her.

"Okay," she says, lightly clapping her hands. "Open your eyes and take a deep breath." I comply. I smile, a smile that's probably less convincing than my robotic affirmation voice, but she can only expect so much.

"I think we made some real progress today," she says.

I'm not so sure, but I automatically nod in agreement. "I think so, too."

"So, tell me about this date," she says in a voice that I can't distinguish between concerned therapist and gossiping BFF. "What's this Prince Charming's name?"

Chapter 15

TWO DECIMAL POINTS JEANETTE

I have a lot of trouble sleeping that night. Every time I finally get one footling thought to leave my head, a new one sneaks in. I fight for sleep in a half-awake stupor until the sun comes up and I accept that sleep is impossible at this point. I get up and realize it's only 7 a.m., abnormally early for me, and immediately drive to the gym to clear my head. Maybe I can run myself to sleep. The weather is finally turning toward favorable outdoor running conditions. In my sleep-deprived state, this doesn't register with me until I walk *inside*, out of the pleasant early spring air, and see the brightly-colored placard advertising the meeting place for the 7 a.m. "Social Run." I'm too late for the social run, but just in time for the anti-social run.

I promise myself that I'll start group activities next week; I only saw Dr. Kelley yesterday and I need to ease myself into it.

Besides, I only have twenty minutes left on the audiobook version of Neil Gaiman's *The Ocean at the End of the Lane*—just enough treadmill time for a respectable warmup.

It never ceases to amaze me how different the faces of the gym crowd look when I'm not here during one of my normal intervals. I recognize very few of them, which is a plus for me since I have a new fitness ball workout I've been meaning to try for a while. At least this way, no one I know will see me if I look like a total idiot derping about on an inflatable fitness orb. I shove earbuds into the depths of my ear canal the packaging warns against and press the Quick Start button on the treadmill.

Neil Gaiman's soothing narration, the gentle hum of the treadmill, and the steady rhythm of my rapid footfalls does more to calm the loud voices of my inner thoughts than all the relaxation and focusing techniques I tried and failed at the night before. If it weren't for the fact that falling asleep while running at six miles per hour on a treadmill is incredibly dangerous, I could definitely do it right now.

Gone are the plotting thoughts of how I can pull off returning Jeanette's day planner to her, which was by far the most pervasive thought of the night (followed closely by all the freelance work I haven't started but have contracted to complete, the prospect of a second date with Average Joe, and—last but not least—the combination to Joe's iPhone). Twenty minutes go by far faster than it should, and for a second I consider ditching the stability ball workout and just keep going on the treadmill, but one glance over my shoulder at the uncharacteristically empty stretching area pushes this thought away.

I grab the awkward, short-person-sized stability ball—color code silver—coated in a thin film of a thousand other people's sweat and dead skin. Balance is not one of my physiological strengths, and as I situate myself for the first exercise in the routine, simple ball crunches, I cheat a little by wedging my feet under the railing that separates the stretching area from the hard basketball court below (and certain serious injury of inattentive athletes). Even so, I am wobbly as I crunch up.

The next exercise requires me to lie down on my back, feet propped up on top of the ball, repeatedly lifting my ass off the floor—not exactly what I would call a flattering motion. I'm glad Average Joe, or any other marginally attractive man who might care to look for that matter, isn't around on a Sunday at 8 a.m. to see me thrusting my pelvis about in the name of a firmer ass. They must all be in church. On the other hand, since it's taking all my brain power to focus on maintaining my balance and keeping the fitness orb from flying at warp speed into a Stairmaster, I'm not strangled by thoughts of how I'm going to return Jeanette's day planner. I move to the next exercise in the rotation, lying on my back passing the ball between my hands and feet at contrasting intervals. It's not until I lose my grip and send the silver ball bouncing over my head that the unpleasant task re-enters my consciousness.

Jeanette is hosting a baby shower at her house today. I know this because I read it in her day planner: Sunday, March 11, 2:00 p.m.—host baby shower for Amy. Jeanette's address is printed on the inside cover of the day planner, in the event that someone finds it and needs to return it to its rightful owner. Based on this alone, it would not be unreasonable to show up at her house, but it still reeks of a creep factor that makes even my skin crawl a little.

I return home around 10 a.m., which still leaves an inordinate amount of time between now and Jeanette's baby shower. While I should use this time for something productive like sleeping, freelance work, laundry, cleaning behind the refrigerator, or knitting a beanie for a baby I don't know at a shower I haven't been invited to with knitting skills I don't possess, I instead leaf intently through Jeanette's day planner. I tell myself I'm doing it so I can find the right moment in her schedule to return the stolen planner, an open window into her personal life, even though I know deep down I'm just doing it so I can stick my head in this wide-open window and take a good look around.

It's like she does all the things that I would do if I weren't so socially awkward, a complete homebody, and had friends. She has a recurring eyebrow and upper lip wax appointment on the third Wednesday of every month. She has neatly written codes for everything—Wax UL & EB—but these codes are easily decipherable. She could have just written "wax 5 p.m." but no, for some reason she had to be specific. Next month, she has a Groupon for a wine tour out in what passes for wine country in Missour-ah. There is no corresponding code to indicate whether this is a solo or group tour, but she will be part of a gaggle of bitches for "Bach Party—R.A." on April 30. It could be a bachelor, not bachelorette party, based on the abbreviation, but this is unlikely. Even more unlikely that it's actually a party that involves listening to the complete works of Johann Sebastian Bach, though that kind of party would be right up my alley.

I don't feel disturbingly intrusive until I manage to decipher what I can only conclude is the pattern of her menstrual cycle. There is a little number one in the upper right-hand corner somewhere around the second week of each month and in the lower right corner, a set of digits with two decimal points that, upon closer pattern examination, looks like her morning temperature. Is Jeanette trying to get pregnant? Is she trying *not* to get pregnant? I don't even know if Jeanette is dating anyone. Maybe I could return the day planner with the unread book my mother bought for me when I went off to college—*The Fertility Method of Natural Family Planning*. It would certainly see far more practical use from someone else.

The guilt immediately sets in—just from thinking of the book published by the Catholic Church or from knowing I interrupted the tracking of something so important to someone—I'm not sure. Either way, I know there's no way I'll be able to shake it until I return the deeply personal item. I look at the clock and see that the baby shower will be starting in forty-five minutes. I barely have enough time to come up with a decent exit strategy since I just spent the better part of an afternoon trolling through someone else's personal life. Fuck plans, anyway.

I just need to do it and get it over with, like ripping a strip of waxy muslin off an unsuspecting upper lip. I'd never even noticed Jeanette had upper lip hair. I grab my keys and commit Jeanette's address (written neatly inside the front cover of the planner) to memory, plotting the best route to get there from Target before people start showing up for the baby shower. First things first—I need to buy another one of these day planners.

Jeanette's house is at the far end of a cul-de-sac. The farther I drive down the street, the smaller the houses get. Typical for Johnson County—stick the bigger fancier houses more ostentatiously close to the major thoroughfares so more people can see them. The lawn is neatly manicured and adorned in each corner is a tight bunch of pink balloons. *It's a girl.* I don't see any cars in the driveway or parked on the street outside; either Jeanette is parked in the garage or she ran out for something last minute that she forgot for the shower. I hope it's the latter. My resolve is fading quickly and leaving the little black book in the mailbox is sounding more and more appealing by the minute, although I think that might actually be illegal.

In any case, my inner bunch of pink balloons is burst when I spot Jeanette hurrying from room to room through the open blinds that separate us. She is so busy rushing around, it doesn't surprise me when she doesn't see me striding up her driveway. I gather my strength and push the doorbell button before I realize I have no idea what I am going to say. It's now officially too late to drop the book on the doorstep and make a run for it. *Maybe not,* I say to myself as the chiming melody of the doorbell tone echoes in my ears, not a ding-song or buzzing noise, but one of those custom chimes like a grandfather clock. I start to turn away from the door and am so surprised to hear it open behind me that I drop both books—her planner and the empty one I just bought but ran over with my car so it would look used. I'm so bad at this plan to flee that I'd forgotten one crucial step and my subconscious does it for me.

"Ann?" she says in a voice that's appropriately confused.

I manage a smile that I'm sure looks as awkward as I feel. "Hi, Jeanette. Sorry to bother you." I pick up both books and hold the one scuffed by my driver's side tire with my left hand next to my face.

I swallow hard and continue, smiling. "I was just putting something in my day planner today when I realized that it wasn't my day planner; mine was still in the bottom of my gym bag where I left it. Anyway, they look exactly the same and I must have picked yours up by mistake at the gym at some point."

I should give my subconscious credit. For something that was made up entirely on the spot, it sounds completely legit. Jeanette appears to buy it, too, and her eyes move down the length of my right arm to the outstretched hand holding the offending day planner. I keep talking.

"I'm so sorry I didn't notice it before now and I have no idea where I might have picked it up."

"Oh no," Jeanette says, taking the day planner and hugging it to her chest. "It was an honest mistake; I knew I should have gotten something a little more distinctive. I've been looking all over for this thing! I thought I was going crazy retracing my steps over and over. I'd given up hope that I'd ever find it!"

"Again, I'm really sorry," I say.

"No, no. Don't apologize. I'm just glad you returned it. I'm expecting some company in a few minutes but won't you please come in to have some punch as a thank you?"

I'd rather have some punch in the face. "No; I wouldn't want to impose."

"It's no imposition whatsoever."

"Thanks, but I have a lot to do today," I lie. Well, half lie. I *do* have a lot of things I could—and should—be doing today, but I already know I'm not going to do any of them. After I leave here, I'm just going to order takeout and throw myself a nice pity party, hopefully pity party myself to sleep. I could have a second career as a pity party planner; I'm that good at it.

"Are you sure? I've got regular and sugar free," she says. Of course she does. She probably also has gluten-free chips and a vegan variety of French onion dip.

"No, I should really be going."

"Okay, well next week I'm going to buy you a cup of tea as a thank you, and I will not take no for an answer."

"That's not necessary."

"I'm aware of that, but I still won't take no for an answer."

What do you say to someone who won't take no for an answer? Apparently, you can't say no, because I hear myself say "Okay."

"Okay. I work the late shift tomorrow, but what about lunch time?"

When she suggested next week, I thought she'd meant the week after this one which is now only hours old. Is Monday considered the start of the week to some? I guess it could be. I guess I secretly hoped that she'd get caught up in the excitement of the baby shower and forget all about it, but I forgot who I was dealing with. This was temperature-to-two-decimal-points Jeanette who provided regular and sugar-free punch to her house guests. She was probably mentally scrawling the appointment in her newly returned day planner as we speak.

"How about noon?" she asks.

"Umm . . . okay. Noonish."

"Noon. Tomorrow, the Starbucks on Metcalf and Shawnee Mission Parkway."

Just like that, I have a date to have coffee with—a friend. I guess I could call her a friend: a friend who, as of an hour ago, has the same day planner as me. A friend who I often avoid at the gym just so I don't have to talk to anyone. A friend who knows orders of magnitude less about me than I know about her.

Chapter 16

PERSONAL FAKER

I head straight to the community center after my coffee with Jeanette. I prepared for the event by bringing my gym bag, thinking my psyche would be so fragile after this rare social encounter I would need the endorphins to normalize. To my surprise, however, I leave feeling remarkably placid. Jeanette was an easy person to talk to, meaning she spent most of the hour talking about herself, so I didn't have to return the favor. Why can't people be more like Jeanette and just talk about themselves instead of wanting to know everything about me all the time?

I legitimately enjoyed hearing about her three older brothers, all of whom were putting pressure on her to find a special man friend but kept scaring all potential candidates off. She gave me a thorough rundown of the three part time jobs she has—one of which is the community center—because she's been trying to land a full-time gig ever since she left grad school with a master's in communication. I didn't even know that was a field of study, but as she talks, I imagine all the ways I would fail out of it in spectacular fashion. I did my part by listening intently and nodding where appropriate, and was surprised to find the hour passed quickly without the need for a mentally therapeutic workout at the end.

I do, however, need to burn off all those calories I consumed. I drank what had to be the thickest and most sugary beverage I've ever had in my life, only because I ordered the most complicated-sounding thing on the menu in an attempt to sound like I knew what I was doing. What "Annie" ended up getting (seriously–only Starbucks could mess up "Ann") was a chocolate caramel milkshake with the faintest notes of coffee flavoring and cinnamon.

I pull out my toothbrush the minute I enter the women's locker room, not because I personally feel the need to scrub my enamel free of chocolate and/or coffee stains and rotting sugar, but because I have to go in for my four-month cleaning at Dad's office next week (he's had me on the four-month schedule since I was twelve) and somehow, he'll be able to immediately identify the froofy latte damage unless I immediately destroy the evidence. Most of the neon pink, comic sans notices announcing the thief's presence–my presence–have been torn down, but a few stragglers remain on the locker room walls. I wonder if there are matching blue ones in some manly font in the men's locker room . . . in Stencil or Courier New, perhaps.

I've promised myself that I'll start doing the group class thing later this week. I'm going to start slow, with yoga. Although I have nothing to base this decision on, it sounds like the class with the lowest barrier to entry. Today, though, is another circuit training day–more mountain climbers, planks, burpees, pushups, squats, and other exercises I routinely have nightmares about. Still, I've gotten much better at it since I started. Like the big motivational poster of a sunset runner in silhouette mounted in the upstairs family restroom says, "It never gets easier. You just get better."

I find a section of the free weights area I can claim as my own little bubble and set up all the things I'll need for my hour of circuit training: the orange dumbbells (eight pounders), purple dumbbells (twelve pounders), resistance bands, sliders for my feet, a Bosu ball, jump rope, and a box for squat jumps. The things I need two of, I can only find one of. I spend a good three minutes that should be devoted to the start of my warmup wandering around the gym trying in vain to find the missing twin of the equipment I need. By the time I give up and decide to start my first circuit, I'm agitated enough that a folded pair of socks I spot in a corner with *Green Eggs and Ham* printed on them looks like an appealing item to take home, but I successfully ignore it.

I'm halfway through my first circuit (two minutes running in place, one minute pushups, two minutes jumping jacks, one minute squats, two minutes jump rope, one minute mountain climbers with sliders, well, one slider) when I spot two familiar faces across the track over in the weight room. One is Joe, the other is a guy I also see in here a lot. He's built like Gunther the Grunter and dresses in similar workout attire, but I've never heard him do the obnoxious grunting thing. I have seen him pull off some ridiculous feats of strength and agility that would make me not only grunt but scream and possibly die. At the moment, he's doing squat jumps, not just onto a box that stands at waist height, but onto an upside-down Bosu ball on top of a box that stands at waist height, all without the slightest trace of strain or fatigue.

I look down at my personal hoard of circuit training equipment at the squat jump box I use, which comes up just to my knees and makes me feel immediately inadequate. Still, I remind myself, his workouts only seem easy because as soon as he's done with an exercise, he takes a long break to go talk to someone about improving his or her (but usually her) form. True to character, he's no sooner abandoned his mongoose-like set of squat jumps than he's chatting up my old pal Skinny Bitch, who's not performing her lat pull downs to a degree that meets his high standards. He's like a fake personal trainer—a personal faker. He's living proof that you can get totally ripped by doing a one-hour workout in four hours' time, and without grunting your way to muscular fortitude.

By the time I huff and puff into my third circuit (two minutes standing mountain climbers, one minute high plank, two minutes burpees, one minute squat jumps, two minutes ski jumps, one minute side plank), I've only seen The Personal Faker do three exercises *total*. He has, however, carried on what looked like some heavy conversation with five different women, correcting kettlebell form, plank form, squat form, you name it. This guy's the most self-proclaimed expert I've ever seen. Meanwhile, I've already managed to burn over 300 calories, according to my monitor watch. I wonder how many calories talking out your ass for an hour burns. Jeanette and the Personal Faker should become special man-and-lady friends; they'd never run out of things to talk about. Jeanette's brothers might even be too intimated by the Personal Faker to disapprove.

Joe, on the other hand, is just finishing up the bench press portion of his weights workout, which has transpired at the pace of a normal person with better things to do, including a day job that remains, to date, a mystery. As I end my third circuit followed by one minute of rest, The Personal Faker ends his brief encounter with the triceps contraption that resembles an old man's ball sack, and Joe ends his bench press, the three of us converge near the water fountain. The Personal Faker makes eye contact with me and before I can look away, he's pulling one earbud out so that he can dispense what I assume is going to be his expert mansplained opinion on my burpee form. *You're right,*

I think to myself. *It does suck. It sucks because burpees suck and will to live is directly correlated with proper burpee form.*

"Hey, I didn't see you over there," Joe says with a hand that starts to move toward touching my arm, but changes its mind halfway through.

"Quick, pretend you're talking to me," I say, dividing my gaze between Average Joe and The Personal Faker.

Joe looks confused. "Um, I *am* talking to you. I don't have to pretend."

I lock my eyes with his and smile a smile that probably looks fake, but still elicits a reciprocal response from him. I let myself drown in his smile and my own little streams of sweat, which I feel converge into a tributary between my boobs. I hope he can't tell that my cleave sweat thing is happening, but I do hope he can tell that I just brushed my teeth.

"Right, of course you are. Hi!"

"Hi," he says. The Personal Faker shoves his earbud back in and breaks right, toward the water fountain, as though that was his intention all along. "How are you?"

"Fine! Good." *Sweaty. Stinky. I hate burpees and I feel like I might collapse and die.*

"Good," he says, inviting an awkward pause that finds both of us nodding at one another and trying to think of something to say. He succeeds first.

"So, I had a good time the other night. Did you?"

"Yes, me too. It was fun. Sorry I was so . . . anxious." *Also, antisocial and kleptomaniac.*

"Nah, it's okay. I was nervous, too. Still coming to dodgeball Thursday?"

Crap. Dodgeball. Same night as yoga, the first group class I am going to try as part of my overturning of new leaves. I make a mental note to check the schedule to make sure I can squeeze both in.

"Absofruitly I am," I say in complete disbelief that I just said that word that isn't even a word. Who is this sweaty spaz demon who has possessed my body?

"We have the super late game this week, 9:15. I was going to text you but it's been a busy week and I forgot. I hope that's okay."

Yesssss! I *can* fit in both yoga and dodgeball. At least dodgeball will give me the vigorous workout I'll miss out on in yoga. "Yeah, that should work just fine."

"The guys probably won't want to go out afterwards with it being so late on a week night, but if you'd like to go with just me, maybe we can go grab a drink together? You still willing to be seen in public with me again?"

I've got the stamp of approval from my therapist and I went with another human being for coffee today. "Yes, I think I am."

"Great. See you then." With that, he strides to the water fountain before either of us can say an awkward "goodbye for now." I need to grab a drink of water too, but the Personal Faker has posted up near there. Instead I turn back to my circuit training area, where someone has since infiltrated my bubble and taken the slider I needed for the last exercise of my fourth and final circuit. I need two, I had one, and now I have none. I look around for something else I can use under my feet to do my sliding lunges, the only exercise that stands between me and thighs that rub together when I walk. Once again, I spot the pair of *Green Eggs and Ham* socks. I jog over and pick them up, look around to make sure no one's looking before I smell them from a safe distance. They smell clean enough, not that it matters since I'm about to get them very dirty.

After I finish my final circuit, I meticulously scrub all my equipment down with Sani-wipes and return everything to its proper place. All the sliders are still missing; an empty cubby in the equipment cabinet stares back at me and I worry that no one will know where they're supposed to go. Finally, I shake out the socks free of the big dust bunnies they collected on the floor when I used them as a circuit training aid. They're going straight in the wash when I get them home.

As much as I hate the circuit training—it's so strenuous and I never want to do it—I always feel like a total badass when I finish it and today's no exception. As per usual, though, I feel like I could get my money's worth at an all you can eat buffet. I award myself double food indulgence points for managing to avoid the intrusion of The Personal Faker. I just might spring for a double slice of red velvet from The Cheesecake Factory tonight. Besides, the latte-shake "Annie" drank didn't really count.

Feeling satisfied with myself, I don't even step on the scale in the locker room, and instead go straight to the combination lock that separates me from my gym bag, ignoring the bright pink PSA taped to my locker. I don't pause to throw the socks in my bag, as it would only put one more obstacle in my path to FOOD. If I'm ever independently wealthy, I'm going to hire someone whose only job is to bring me food at the exact moment I emerge from the shower after a workout. Until then, the hostess at The Cheesecake Factory will have to endure my stench.

My badass hanger reverie is rudely interrupted as Remy the security guard greets me in the hallway.

"Hello, Miss Josephson. Good workout today?"

I am suddenly half as famished as I was two seconds ago. "Yes."

"Your socks got really dirty," he says, eyeballing the wadded socks in my right hand.

I look down. "Oh, these? I actually found them upstairs. I was just going to drop them at the lost and found on my way out."

Chapter 17

DEBBIE DOWNWARD DOG

My calendar reminds me that the day I pinpointed for starting group classes at the community center is finally here. I feel like the date circled in red is taunting me, just daring me to find an excuse from my usual array of excuses to chicken out, but I can't think of a reason good enough to put it off any longer. I've already spent so much time preparing, both mentally and financially, that it would be a shame to chicken out now.

Through the first half of the week, I did enough freelance work to pay for the yoga gear that I found to be astonishingly expensive when I ventured out to Dick's Sporting Goods. Despite what my parents said at our last awkward dinner, I now believe I am definitely in the wrong business. Apparently, all you have to do to turn an immediate profit in life is buy some cheap exercise gear, throw the "yoga" label on it, and charge twice as much. Case in point:

Barely opaque black exercise pants: $24.99
Even less opaque black yoga pants: $54.99
Purple exercise mat with no pattern: $7.99
Purple yoga mat with bamboo pattern: $19.99
Lump of foam: $4.99
Yoga block: $12.99
Geriatric gait belt: $10.99
Yoga strap: $17.99
Gardening gloves, fingers intact: $2.99
Fingerless yoga gloves: $12.99
Six-pack of socks: $6.99
Toe socks: Please take them and I will give you $2.99
One pair of weird yoga toe socks: $6.99

Despite hearing repeated litanies on the virtues of yoga—mind, body, spirit, menstrual cycle—I've never attempted it. I'm simultaneously intimidated by it and driven to eye rolling at all the metaphysical chi bullshit. It's just stretching, right? How hard can it be? This is why it's my first group class attempt. I'm in such good shape I'm bound to look at least as competent as half the people in there. Naturally, in the course of my gym time I've also found that the best way to fool people into thinking you know exactly what you're doing is to have the gear to back it up. Add this to the intimidation factor, and I just end up buying all of the things. I'm sure I don't need all this crap for my first yoga class ever, but at least I'll look the part.

Donning my yoga pants, gloves, socks, and skintight top, carrying a canvas tote bag with my yoga straps and blocks over one shoulder, gripping my shiny new purple yoga mat with bamboo pattern under the other, I walk into the semi-darkened room as though I am an expert at stretching and metaphysical chi bullshit. To my surprise, there are at least a couple people in the room with more yoga accessories than me. One is your standard John-son County soccer mom looking type, the other is a man–the only one in the room. I pick a spot with plenty of personal space, but it is soon invaded by stragglers shuffling into class one min-ute before it's supposed to start. I take a deep breath, remind myself that part of all this nonsense is to step out of my comfort zone, and tell myself to get over it.

Everyone else is either sitting criss-cross-apple-sauce in the middle of their mats or stretching, so I decide to do a little of both and sit on my mat stretching my arms so I can twist around and survey the rest of the class. There is still just the one guy, tucked into an enviable far back corner in the sea of estrogen. Half the women in the class are trying to inconspicuously identify the fattest lady in class and breathing sighs of relief when they dis-cover it's not them. The other half are women whose yoga pants show off how bulge- and cellulite-free their bodies are. Once such woman softly pads her way to an empty mat at the front of the room and identifies herself as the instructor in a soft voice.

"My name's Mary and I'm your Thursday night instructor. Is this anyone's first time to yoga?"

I don't raise my hand. *Look at all this yoga shit; obviously this ain't my first rodeo.*

"In our last few seconds before we start class, why don't you go ahead and introduce yourself to your neighbors."

I stiffen as hands outstretch into my already abbreviated per-sonal space. I smile and shake each one mechanically. Ann. Ann. Ann. Ann. I remember only one name spat at me, the neighbor directly in front of me, sporting the same purple bamboo yoga mat as mine, but a lot less shiny and presumably with an aroma that is less eau de plastique fraîche, more sweaty feet.

She exclaims, "Hi! I'm Debbie." *You'll be seeing a lot of my perfect ass in the next hour.*

The instructor interrupts my rising anxiety. "Let's start in a comfortable seat with some deep, cleansing breaths."

Everyone around me inhales at a socially unacceptable decibel level then exhales with an exaggerated sigh that makes me open my eyes, then I wonder if I was supposed to be closing my eyes in the first place. I glance around. Yes. Eyes closed. I join the party for the second "deep, cleansing breath" and, much like the deep breathing exercises Dr. Kelley taught me to do when I feel anxiety coming on, I feel an immediate slowing of my heart rate and a calm wash over me. *So, this is yoga, huh? Even with all the overpriced gear, it's still a hell of a lot cheaper than therapy.* The instructor continues in the same voice Dr. Kelley uses when we do our visualizations.

"Just begin to let go of your day. As you deepen your breath, I want you to think about setting an intention for your practice today. Why are you here?"

My day has consisted of ice cream for breakfast and less than an hour's worth of actual work, so I have little trouble letting go of it. I'm here because my therapist told me to be here, so I am relieved when I discover this is a rhetorical question being answered only by more melodramatic breathing and, from Debbie's mat in front of me, almost sexual-sounding sighs that make me peek out of an open sliver of one eye.

"Let's rise and take our first vinyasa." I have no idea what that means, but I take my cues from the instructor and the bodies around me and inhale exaggeratedly as I stand and sweep my arms overhead.

"Swan dive forward fold, plank, chaturanga, cobra or up dog, everyone meets in downward facing dog," she says with what feels like a fraction of a second—which is less than as far behind as I am from everyone else—between each word, only one of which I understand. Still, I manage to mimic the movements around me until I'm staring down the polka-dot underwear I can see through Debbie's yoga pants as she downward dogs in front of me. I mimic the position and I'm so busy looking around me that I don't notice the instructor until her hands are on my lower back shifting my weight backward for me. I jump instinctively which only amplifies the pre-existing tightness in my calves. I feel the blood rush to my head and can only imagine the shade of red it must be turning at the moment. Although I am less than well-endowed in the breast department, I am barely an inch away from being able to self-motorboat.

By the third vinyasa, I'm moving in step with everyone else and once again feel like I look like I know what I'm doing. *This shit is easy.*

"Right leg lifts to the sky, bring it through, rise up for Warrior I," the instructor continues. I follow the sequence, watching Debbie the whole way since the instructor has decided to stop doing the sequence herself and instead softly murmur orders as she watches everyone else's form. I'm thankful Debbie's polka-dotted ass knows what it's doing, and is less visible in this position, which I must say makes me feel nothing like a warrior as I struggle to gain my balance, wobbling back and forth, side to side.

I find myself sweaty and out of breath as we move through the poses, which I did not expect having gone into this class thinking it'd be all stretching and sleepytime poses. I work out every damned day. I ran over four miles yesterday. I'm not supposed to be out of breath in yoga. At the end of every pose, the instructor adds an "if you want a little more challenge" aside that everyone else in class accepts with gusto and I attempt, badly. One minute, we're in Warrior II pose (how many warriors are there in yoga, anyway?), the next minute, despite the fact that my thighs are visibly quivering from holding this position, we're wrapping one arm around our bent knee and the other behind our backs, trying to get our palms to touch one another.

"Listen to your body and do what feels good for you. Remember your body is yours and not your neighbor's; that's why we call it practice instead of competition. Don't even look at your neighbor; look inward and don't forget to breathe." I choose to believe she's not talking to me, and unglue my eyes from Debbie Downward Dog in front of me, all twisted up like a pretzel and making it look easy, not even breaking a sweat. A muscle in my left lower back screams at me to back off, but I'm so close to getting the very edge of my fingertips to touch when the instructor, as if hearing the scream, rescues me. Just in time, too, I can feel a fart trying to escape from all the twisting midsection work. No one else wants to listen to my body.

"Release your warrior and move into child's pose for three cleansing breaths. After your third inhale, move into squat position preparing for crow pose." I have no idea what any of these things are but I am pleased to discover that child's pose involves resting my head on my new-plastic-smelling mat. I've learned that cleansing breaths mean loud exhaling sighs and my mat reflects them right back in my face. I'm still trying not to fart.

"Now move into crow pose or stay in child's pose if you need more time. Just listen to your body." I want more time, but I'm not going to give her or anyone else around me the satisfaction. Besides, everyone else in the class has already raised themselves up into a childbirthing squat (not that I'm looking at my neighbors). I watch as Debbie Downward Dog bends her elbows and hops her feet off the mat at the same time, resting her knees just above her elbows. I try to do the same, and immediately fall back to the floor in favor of toppling in the opposite direction, directly into her perfectly executed and inexplicably solid crow pose. The instructor even thinks so.

"Beautiful, Debbie!" she exclaims then quickly backtracks. "Beautiful, all of you. Wherever you are right now is exactly where you're supposed to be," she says. As if on cue, as I attempt to lift my second foot off the floor, my hips shift under me and I topple to the floor. *If this is exactly where I'm supposed to be, can I just sit here in a pile until "practice" is over?* The fart escapes, but it does so at a decibel level that I am convinced is only audible to me over the sound of all the loud breathing. I wait for the invisible stink cloud to rise from the gasses but thankfully it does not. I wonder whether I'm supposed to retry crow pose or if this is like a staring contest I've been eliminated from. *You win, Debbie.*

I glance at my heart rate monitor watch and see that fifty-five minutes have gone by. I've managed to make it through almost the entire class; it would be stupid to give up now, especially when I always try to finish strong—mostly to justify dessert later.

"Great job, everyone. Now let's move onto our backs for our final savasana." I watch as everyone lies like corpses on their mats. This is not my idea of finishing strong. I immediately feel myself beginning to nod off, so despite direct orders from the instructor, I start thinking. I have a dodgeball game in an hour, then I'm supposed to go out with Joe for a drink. If I feel half dead after an hour of yoga, how dead am I going to feel after dodgeball? I should cancel the date—er, drinks—with Joe. Or give him a rain check. If I do that, will I be the bitch who blew him off? More than I probably already am? I'll at least have to shower after dodgeball . . . good God, this mat smells like formaldehyde. Maybe that's why we end class in corpse pose.

I'm shaken from my thought spiral by Yogi Mary's voice.

"Begin to awaken and make your way up to a comfortable seat." The guy in the corner is already there; the second fattest girl in class is asleep next to him. I sit up, anxious to get out of here before Mary has a chance to thank me for attending class or learn my name, or for Debbie Downward Dog to give me some pointers on my form, like the female version of the Personal Faker.

"As you go out into the world," instructor Mary speak-sings, "take your practice with you. Come back to your intention throughout the rest of your day and let it guide you." In spite of myself, I think of my prescribed intention, to socialize myself like a rescued shelter dog. I can do that for the rest of the day. In fact, it's the only thing I actually have to do.

"Bring palms to touch," her voice continues. I assume the pretend prayer motion I'm well-versed in. "And know that you are enough. You are perfect just the way you are. The highest and brightest in me honors the highest and brightest in you. Namaste."

Everyone bows, so I follow suit. As I do, I notice that the muscle in my lower back, the one that has been increasingly aggravated the more I circuit train, is no longer complaining. I feel . . . I search for the word . . . good. I actually feel *good*, and I didn't even need to steal anything to feel that way. Of course, my head also feels swirly and dehydrated.

People begin standing, thanking the instructor, rolling up their mats, and chatting with one another. I roll up mine quickly and sloppily, counting the number of steps to the door as I do so. I dart out quickly, making my way downstairs to hide in a locker room shower until either the hot water runs out or I have to go play dodgeball.

As good as I feel, I'm not sure I can return to something that I am so inadequate at again. I hate doing things I'm not good at; it's why I don't go find a full-time job doing something more challenging, date more guys, or do things like yoga. The stupid motivational poster is right, but I don't want to get better;

I just want life to get easier. I count it as a victory that I actually branched out instead of chickening out—even if it was on my doctor's orders—but I'm pretty sure yoga, which must be Sanskrit for "room full of people trying not to fart for an hour," is not the class for me.

Chapter 18

GOLIATH AND THE COBRA KAI-CLOPS

I sweat a lot more onto my pretty new yoga clothes than I'd anticipated. Who goes into yoga expecting to exert themselves? As I dig to the bottom of my gym bag, I am crushed by the realization that I now must choose between playing dodgeball in the yoga clothes that smell like department store and body odor, or the last-resort workout outfit I keep in the bottom of my bag for when I've put off laundry for too long—which I have. It consists of a pair of running shorts that ride up into my crotch joints at the slightest movement and an ill-fitting Crest t-shirt my dad got me at one of his dental conferences. I sigh audibly as I opt for the undesirable yet non-smelly ensemble. After all, I'm just there to play dodgeball; who cares what I'm wearing, right?

I repeat this fallacious mantra to myself even as I break out my curling iron to make a ponytail that will be pretty by comparison. If they're looking at my fabulous hair, they won't be paying any attention to my stupid t-shirt or my constant tugging at my shorts to cover my thighs. The same thighs whose color currently resembles the snow outside that's been sticking around since January and is finally starting to melt. I even smear a fresh, shiny coat of Skittles-flavored lip gloss across my mouth and pop a Tic-Tac—just in case.

I nearly wet the running shorts that are already riding up as I exit the locker room and find Average Joe waiting for me.

"I didn't mean to scare you," he says as I catch my breath. "I saw you run in there a while ago and wanted to make sure I got this to you before the game."

He hands me a black t-shirt rolled up like a diploma. As I take it from his hand, I feel the urge to shake his free one and smile for an invisible camera off-stage. I don't. Instead, I immediately unroll it and feel my heart sink. I have the exact same t-shirt at home in Room 403. I saw it one night as I was on my way out the door and liked it. The torso-length logo on the front is the Cobra Kai logo (except the cobra's teeth hold a bright orange dodgeball) from *The Karate Kid*, which happens to be one of my favorite movies of all time. I always had a thing for Ralph Macchio; well, both him and William Zabka. This means that the t-shirt I have at home belongs to someone on the team. Someone on *my* team. On the other hand, this one is a lot closer to my size, so I could always drop the other one in the lost and found and self-flagellate 100 lashes if I needed to atone for my guilt. I look up to see a smiling Joe and force a smile of my own.

"We didn't wear them last week because no one had done their laundry. Plus, I said there was a chance we might have a new team member and I didn't want you to feel left out. But now that you're officially part of the team . . ." he trails off.

"The 'Sweep the Ball, Johnny' team?" I say, turning the logo around to face him.

He laughs, which comes with the smile that has infiltrated my dreams. "Yeah, that was kind of my idea. I'm a big *Karate Kid* fan."

No fair. Me too. "Thank you." I hug the still-warm t-shirt to my chest. "What do I owe you for it?"

He addresses me with a dismissive wave. "Nothing, please. It's a gift."

"From everyone?"

"Well, from me. But from everyone by proxy. There's no 'me' in team, right?"

"I don't think that's how that phrase goes."

"Right. Well, anyway, don't feel like you have to wear it if you don't want to."

"No," I say. Like I'd rather wear a t-shirt that advertises something as sexy as dental hygiene and stick out like the sore thumb I somehow gave myself in crow pose. "I'm going to go put it on right now." I feel like I'm blushing. I tell my brain to tell my face to stop blushing and turn back to the locker room, making sure my curly ponytail flounces as I do so. Is this flirting? I'm not a flirter . . . not a good one, anyway.

The Cobra Kai color scheme doesn't go with my strawberry banana yoga pants, so I decide to stick with the running shorts that ride up. Also, I'm convinced some farticles might be embedded in the seat. You'd think that for pants that expensive, the yoga apparel magnates would use fabric that doesn't hold a stink. The team t-shirt has the new shirt softness to it, unspoiled by washing machines (unlike the same version of the shirt I have at home, which I often wear lounging around the apartment because of its inherent softness). It's a little snug, but hugs my body in all the places I try so hard to maintain in this building five to seven days a week. The fabric is warm and the pressed logo and letters are still sticky—Joe probably came straight here from the t-shirt shop and rolled it up so the screen press wouldn't stick to itself. I press the corners of the logo stretched across my boobs to make sure they're secure right as one of the Gladyses from senior water aerobics walks in. She pretends not to notice that I'm feeling myself up. *At least I don't floss my business with a towel while everyone's watching.* Besides, I have a flirty ponytail. Mind yourself, Gladys.

As we make our way to the court to greet the rest of the team, Joe and I brush hands almost imperceptibly. Since the thumbs of both hands are tucked into the hem of my shorts to keep them from riding up, it speaks to how close he walks next to me. Normally, such close contact would trigger my internal threat level up a color or two; does this mean I'm getting used to having him around? How can I feel this comfortable around a guy I barely know, a guy I've repeatedly stolen from? I'm not even this comfortable around the people I really know, not that that's a wide circle . . .

I don't have time to finish processing this thought as the team comes into view and my brain foists another, far more unpleasant thought upon me. One of these people had to get a replacement team shirt because I stole it from her. Him. Him or her. I mentally measure each team member against my memory of the version of the shirt I have at home, as much as I can do so without being painfully obvious. No one's shirt, besides mine, looks exceptionally new enough to tip me off as the replacement. Based on size alone, I narrow the field down to two people, neither of whom has said more than two words to me, which makes me wonder why. It could also be the pregnant lady, pre-KTFU, whom I have not yet met. Granted, I haven't exactly done my part to engage everyone in conversation, particularly these two shy individuals whose names I am sure I learned at one point but was too distracted to remember. Do they somehow *know* that I am the kind of degenerate who steals people's team t-shirts?

The distraction impacts my performance in the dodgeball game, which is far less all-star worthy than it was last week. I still manage to get two people out and my glasses don't get knocked off my face, but the other team is good. Our teammate Mike isn't as lucky as me. A monster of a man on the other team launches one right at his head during the second match (the only one we win), which hits an unsuspecting Mike smack dab in his left eye socket. He must sit on the sideline with an ice pack like a Cyclops—a Cobra Kai-clops—for the rest of the game. He's the only one to get the Goliath out in any of the four matches we play. I dodge his firebombs only to hear them slam against the back wall like a gunshot, not that I know what gunshots sound like. I live in Johnson County.

"No ball shots to the head!" the ref whistles with an exaggerated "you're out" thumb. I try not to giggle, but am grateful for the distraction from thinking about Shirty 1 and Shirty 2.

The whole game takes less than twenty minutes, half of which is spent tugging at my shorts to keep them from resembling apparel more suited for beach volleyball, and the team leaves with an unexpected level of elation, high-fiving each other on the way out, despite the defeat and not even breaking a sweat. Guess I should be glad I did yoga. Average Joe and I stand at arms' length in front of one another.

"Sorry we lost," I say, not knowing what else to say.

"Nah, it's okay," he says, brushing my ponytail off my right shoulder. *So, he did notice it.* "We lose to them every time we play. Those guys are insane. I think they go to some dodgeball Navy Seal training or something."

"That gigantic guy over there," I say, pointing to Goliath. "Does he always throw that hard?"

"Who, Tony Danza? Yeah. He always throws that hard. I took a shot to the kidney from that guy once and was worried I'd be pissing blood the next day. Good job dodging his shots tonight. Sadly, it's the best you can hope for."

I look over at the guy. He does kind of look like Tony Danza. A really tall, really muscular Tony Danza. Does Average Joe make up code names for everyone in the gym, too? Does he have a code name for me? Ann-acid, maybe. Or worse . . . Ann-gina.

"Is Mike's eye going to be okay?" I ask, trying not to think about Shirty 1, Shirty 2, the Gladyses in the locker room, Goliath, aka Tony Danza, or Joe thinking up code names for me and everyone else in the community center.

"I'm sure he'll be fine." There's an awkward period of silence before he continues. "Did you still want to go get a drink? I know it's late, and it's a school night, but . . ." he trails off again.

"Of course," I say, checking the status of my Skittles lip gloss with my tongue before I continue. "Let me just call my mom and make sure I can be out this late on a school night."

He shoots me an almost horrified look.

"Kidding! Yes, I do. Should I . . . change?" How am I supposed to know what one wears to a dive bar on a second sort-of date?

"No, you don't have to," he says. "I was just gonna throw on a pair of jeans, but only because it's cold out."

Jeans, of course. Glad my duffel bag includes a pair of jeans that don't make me look too deformed. "Okay. Then I'll do the same. Let me just put on my jeans, then. I'll meet you by the front doors."

My muscles are so tired from yoga and dodgeball that I say a silent prayer that I can manage to put my jeans on without face-planting into a locker.

Chapter 19

SPROTS

In addition to the jeans, I put on my regular bra and toss the sweaty sports bra in my duffel bag. The toothpaste t-shirt and bike shorts I throw in the trash. It feels good to get rid of something I don't like and don't use for a change. I have no shortage of workout clothing; however, I unfortunately can't wear most of it to the gym on the off chance people recognize their missing apparel on the wrong body. The jeans, though, are 100 percent mine, and the fit is something that I can tell doesn't go unnoticed by Average Joe, even if he does his best to keep his interest inconspicuous.

"One of these days," he says, holding my coat up while I wriggle myself into the sleeves. Perfect gentleman, as usual. "I'm going to take you on a real date. I promise."

"Why isn't this a real date?" I ask, walking through the door he holds open for me.

"I mean the kind of date where I pick you up at your house and come to your door and we go do something you enjoy doing instead of me picking generic things to do with you shot-in-the-dark style."

I lower my head so he won't see me blushing. "You didn't say 'place of residence' this time."

"No, but I'm being presumptuous saying 'house.' You could live in a cardboard box for all I know."

"Nah," I say. "It's a drywall box. Very classy."

"Well next time, my carriage will arrive at the front door of your drywall box. Since we're doing something generic now, I'll have plenty of time to figure out what you actually like to do over beer," he says, this time holding the passenger door of the car. I wish he'd quit doing that. I can open doors for myself; I have years of experience. He wants to know what I like to do (besides stealing things from strangers, I imagine), but I don't even know what I like to do, except maybe open my own doors.

He must have put on his Zeppelin-scented man spray between dodgeball and now. I can smell it as it wafts over from the driver's seat and makes me want to lean in and take in a deep, cleansing yoga breath. But I don't. That would be weird. I can't believe I didn't pick up on the scent before our last date, which I do think was a real date. Then again, it's not like he'd douse himself in body spray to go work out. Only d-bags like The Personal Faker do shit like that.

JJ's bar is significantly more crowded than it was the last time I went here after dodgeball, which I find jarring until I realize that unlike last time, it's not 6 p.m. and there is a basketball game on. Joe and I are the only two people in the bar who aren't decked out in Kansas Jayhawk red and blue or Kansas State Wildcat purple. I've never felt more conspicuous wearing charcoal gray and jeans in my life. Isn't shooty-hoops season over yet? I feel like the obnoxiousness that accompanies March Madness began eight months ago.

Joe takes my hand in his own and confidently walks the two of us to the end of the bar, right by the jukebox, where there are two lone, unoccupied bar stools.

"Hey, Joe," the bartender nods our way in acknowledgement, temporarily ignoring the clamoring hoops fans who have been waiting their turn for a drink for what I'm guessing is an inordinate amount of time, based on the dirty looks they shoot in our direction. "What'll it be?"

"Two Boulevard Wheats, please," he hollers back to the bartender. To me, in a voice more conducive to close, face-to-face communication, "You haven't stopped liking it, have you?" His lips part into the winning smile that has haunted my dreams for the better part of a month.

"No," I say. I can't help but crack a smile back, despite feeling uneasy between all the annoyed Jayhawk and Wildcat faces on me and the shrunken personal space bubble they're forcing me to occupy. I look to them, then look back to Joe, trying to block them out. I nod in the direction of the bartender.

"They must really like you here," I say with my forced smile.

He must sense my unease because he turns to discern what I was looking at, meeting the angry stares of a crowd of thirsty fans before turning back and giving my wringing hands a reassuring pat.

"Who, this bozo?" he asks within earshot of the bartender who sets the pair of squat bottles in front of us. "He just wants me for my money. Get those mobsters a bucket of these on me, will ya?"

He turns again to the sea of faces sporting angry stares. "Sorry, guys. Next round's on me. Enjoy yourselves."

The tense atmosphere shifts and I can feel myself relax a little bit, letting out the breath I didn't realize I'd been holding. "That's really generous of you."

He takes a drink and his face immediately flushes. "I'm a lover, not a fighter. Sorry about this; I didn't realize there was a game tonight. I don't really pay attention to shooty-hoops."

"You and me both," I say, letting the cold liquid wash away the lump in my throat. "We must be the only two people in Kansas who didn't get the memo."

"Do you wanna go somewhere else?"

"No, that's okay. You like this place and they know you here." *And every other bar would probably be exactly the same.*

"You sure?"

I nod, opening my mouth to say something but am pre-emptively drowned out by an eruption of cheers from the bar's patrons.

When the noise dies down, Joe asks, "So you're not into sports either then, huh?"

"Nope," I say, shouting over the obnoxious people shouting behind me. "But it's not from a lack of trying, I promise. My dad, he's into every sport in the book and he tried to get me into it, too. It just never took."

"I had a completely different experience. My father didn't take 'team sprots' seriously," he says. I eyeball him curiously before he says "Yes, my father actually called it 'sprots'. Always pushed me to more individual type things, like track and golf. At least your dad tried. Maybe all his trying turned you off."

"Maybe." The conversation halts and we find ourselves awkwardly looking away from one another to the game on the TVs that neither of us is interested in, sipping our beers.

"So, what *are* you into?" he asks. "Music? Books? Movies?"

I try to think. The last concert I went to was Blink-182 more than five years ago, and I'm not willing to admit to any guilty pleasures just yet. Most of the books I have are graphic design books my parents get me as gifts because they have no idea what else to get me besides money. I wish they'd just give me money (well, more money). I have yet to crack the spine on any of them. Three of them are currently propping up my monitor. I go to maybe one movie a year and pick a show time that is guaranteed to yield an empty theater because being around a crowd of strangers in the dark gives me panic attacks, kind of like how I am starting to feel right now.

"No, not really," I say, smiling back at him.

"Well you must be into something."

"Why?"

"Everyone's into something."

Sure, I'm into something. I'm into stealing people's personal items and making up stories about how they use them in their everyday lives, but I'm pretty sure he doesn't want to hear about that. "I'm into exercising. It's why I'm always at the gym."

"That's not a thing you can be into," he says.

"Sure it is."

"Well, if you don't mind my saying so, you don't need it."

I can feel my face flushing and I don't know how to take his statement, other than that I know he's giving me a compliment. Thanks to my mother, I've been rendered completely incapable of handling compliments that aren't back-handed in some way. I need to change the subject before the conversation devolves into him talking about how sexy my ass is, even if it's true, thanks to these jeans and all the woman-hours I've put into the project.

"What about you?" I ask.

He pauses and takes a swig off the bottle, never once breaking eye contact with me. If he knows I'm dodging the question, he doesn't press the issue. Hopefully he assumes I'm just being coy, not that I actually have zero hobbies. "You really wanna know?"

"Why wouldn't I? Is it creepy? Are you into collecting doll

heads or something?" I ask, secretly hoping that behind the gorgeous smile, the generous spirit, the friendly demeanor, there is some sinister character flaw that can bring him down to my level.

"No, no," he says. "It's nothing like that. I build model trains."

"Model trains? What are you, twelve? That's cute."

"Hey now," he says, crossing his arms over his chest. "It's not cute. It's a very masculine hobby."

I giggle silently behind my beer.

"I was always into trains, even as a kid. I always said I wanted to grow up and be a railroad engineer but it just wasn't in the cards for me."

"Why not?"

He smiles. "That's a conversation for another time. I'm not bitter or anything. I made a career for myself and I'm happy with the way things turned out."

I stiffen, sensing the conversation drifting into *what do you do?* territory. "I don't want to know, remember?"

"Right," he says. "We're not our jobs. Or in your case, we're not our jobs or our hobbies, since yours is a lame one."

I'm about to protest when an ear-splitting shattering of glass erupts behind us and everyone falls silent, except for the two opposing fans at the opposite end of the bar who are shouting at one another. Icy air pours in from the broken window behind them. They start lunging at one another.

"Stay here. Don't move," Joe says, briefly putting his hands on my shoulders before darting across the bar and wedging himself between the two fighting men, trying to separate them. As if I could possibly move any muscle in my terrified, catatonic body. Where was this solid state when I needed it in yoga? They keep swinging at one another around Joe's body until I hear him shout over them.

"Police! Break it up, now!"

For a second, everything is silent but for the passing cars on the street outside, which the shivering mass of people inside can now hear distinctly. I briefly entertain the notion that I heard him wrong until I see Joe pull a pair of handcuffs from a holster that was hiding around his right ankle. I feel my spine tingling. I must be in shock. I need one of those beige wool blankets they put around people who are in shock in the movies. Also, it's freezing in here.

A low murmur resumes in the crowd but otherwise everyone is quiet as he handcuffs the two fighters together. He begins to make his way back to me, but he is making eye contact with the bartender. He motions for the bartender to join him and finally turns to me. I'm still shivering and shrinking as far into my corner as I possibly can.

"Sorry, Ann. I'm gonna have to file a report and get an officer here to take these guys to the station. It could take a while. I can have someone take you back to your car if you don't wanna wait."

I move my mouth but no sound comes out. The phrase "scared senseless" comes to mind, but I made out his words just fine so I must not be too shell-shocked.

"S-Someone?" I finally manage to make out.

"Another officer I trust, maybe?"

I shake my head, trying to get the image of me in the seat of a police cruiser out of my mind. "I'll wait. I'm fine."

I wait silently in my little corner of the bar for the better part of two hours, but it feels like mere minutes to me. While Average Joe—Officer Average Joe—files a police report, calls for a squad car to take the fighting fans to the drunk tank, and helps the bartender (who wordlessly keeps my beers coming one right after the other) cover the exposed window with cardboard pieced together from beer cases, I sit and think. And drink. It's like my brain is so busy trying to assimilate this new information that it desperately does not want to fit. The minutes, and empty bottles, pile up before I can even process what's going on.

"Hey Ann, sorry about that." Joe has reappeared at my side. I stare at him blankly. He doesn't want to come into focus. It suddenly occurs to me that I am drunker than I have been in a very long time, possibly ever. I don't want to look drunk.

Joe's iPhone (his new one) rings and I'm temporarily saved. "This is Officer Strong, badge 2036," he answers, holding his index finger up to me, signaling that I'll have to wait a little longer. Instead of a beer, the bartender slides a glass of water in front of me. The jukebox is cycling through Top 40 hits since there's no one left here to pump money into it. So, his last name isn't Willis.

"Sorry again," Joe says, having once again reappeared at my side like magic.

"It's okay," I say. I sound slurry. I repeat myself, trying to sound less slurry and failing.

"Oh, wow," he says, putting his coat around my shoulders. Why didn't he do that two hours ago when I was in shock and freezing my ass off in here and chugging alcohol to stay warm? "You shouldn't drive. You need to let me take you home."

Without a word, I extend my arm so he can help me off the barstool. I wonder how I'll get back to my car tomorrow, but that's the least of my worries at the moment. He deposits me into the passenger seat of his car. On his coat, I detect the familiar Zeppelin scent I can't get enough of. I hope I don't take a deep yoga breath of it. We drive in silence for several minutes before he breaks it, interrupting my train of increasingly disturbing thoughts.

"I'm so sorry that all that happened tonight. I should've taken you somewhere else. You must have been so scared. And they shouldn't have kept serving you drinks. They wouldn't've done that if you hadn't been with me."

"You're a cop," I say after several seconds.

"Um, yep. Yes, I am. I did try to tell you that. A few times."

"You're a cop," I repeat.

"Yes. I'm a cop. You say that like it's a bad thing. You know, I have it on good authority that the ladies have a thing for cops, all men in uniform, really. Or is that just firefighters?"

"You're a cop and that's why they served you drinks immediately."

"Yes, that's why. Now can you please tell me where you live so I can take you home?"

I rattle off my address mechanically and punctuate it with another "You're a cop." *A cop who now knows where I live.*

"And you're drunk. Remind me to tell you everything you said next time we go out."

"Next time?" I say, my drunken tongue tripping over the X sound. "Wait, what did I say?"

"Um, will there not be a next time? Is me being a cop a deal breaker for you?"

You have no idea, I think. "I don't know. You're a cop."

He pulls in front of my building and kills the engine. "I'm going to walk you up just to make sure you get inside okay."

"You can't come in," I snap back. I don't mean for it to come out so clipped and drenched in attitude but it does.

"I won't come in."

"You're a cop."

"Just give me your keys."

He walks me up the stairs which makes my head swirl with each ascending step. At my door, he turns the key in the lock before gently placing the keys back in my hand and clos-ing my fingers around them. I look up at him expecting to see disappointment or disdain, but instead he is smiling. I try to watch with both eyes as his mouth moves up to my forehead and plants a kiss there, but it makes my head all swirly again.

"Get some sleep, Ann. I'll call you tomorrow and get you back to your car."

My heart and head are both pounding as I slip into my apartment through the smallest ajar sliver of door possible. I can't tell if it's from all the new emotions swimming around inside my brain or from climbing all those stairs in my drunken stupor. My eyes focus on the blinking iPhone—Officer Joe Strong's iPhone—on my desk. I grab the phone and shuffle to the spare bedroom, the one that holds all my stolen shit, and shut the door to the room behind me so I can hide.

I curl up in the fetal position on the itchy carpet under me and try to focus my eyes on the lock screen of the phone. I enter 2036 and watch the phone come to life for a couple seconds before my eyelids lose the battle with gravity and I pass out.

Chapter 20

LULU LEMONADE

The stiff carpet of Room 403—which hasn't been vacuumed for months—scratches my face awake the next morning. I'm still in the same semi-fetal position I passed out in. I have a headache. I pick up the phone lying next to me to see what time it is, only to remember that this isn't my phone. It's Joe's phone. Even though it's already after 10 a.m., I squeeze my eyes shut in an effort to will myself back to sleep. But before I can, the previous evening comes flooding back into my memory: the rabid basketball fans, the beer, the fight, the beer, the cop, the beer, the cops, the beer, the ride home, the beer. I also find that I am sore in places that I didn't even know I had muscles, and promise I will never diminish yoga as a fluff workout for JoCo soccer moms again.

A notification pops up on Officer Joe Strong's iPhone; it's the ESPN app notifying him of the score of last night's game. Kansas won by two. I guess he's not *that* nonplussed when it comes to college shooty-hoops after all. It makes me simultaneously wonder what other truths he might have taken liberties with in our conversations, and remind myself that there could be a perfectly legitimate reason he gets score notifications on his phone. After all, he is a red-blooded American male who works in a red-blooded American male dominated profession—as I regrettably learned last night. What else might he be hiding from me? Okay, so he didn't necessarily hide being a police officer, but anyone would agree that it was a bit more than an omission.

I sit up in a shooting panic as another memory from last night enters my consciousness. He drove me home and walked me to my apartment. He knows where I live. He knows which door is mine. He knows my car, Rosa, is sitting at the community center, wondering why I left her all alone overnight. I am never without my car. Even in college, where I was slightly less antisocial than I am now, I never let myself become so incapacitated by alcohol that I was unable to drive myself. On this plane of existence where I can't even control my own compulsions, my car is—or was—the one thing I could always control. I feel lost. I should apologize to Rosa. I decide I have to get back to her as soon as possible, and then start to pick the rest of my ragged self up off the crunchy floor.

Then I once again look down at Joe's phone, wondering what other facts he knows about me, what Ann cards he's holding close to the chest. Maybe he has a police file on me already and it's all sitting there in a neat little folder on his home screen. The temptation is far too great and I decide that whatever regrets I have later can be blamed on my semi-hungover state. I dismiss the ESPN notification with a swipe of the thumb, enter Joe's badge number on the lock screen, and go straight to his email.

It doesn't take me long to discover that Joe doesn't keep work email on his phone; every email is either personal or woefully inane. Joe's mom is passive-aggressively upset with him for missing his grandfather's eighty-fifth birthday. She emailed him the complete text of—not a link to—the local newspaper obituary written up on the grand event. Joe has fourteen cousins on his mom's side and they've been busy making and having babies. Grandpa, whose name was also Joseph, has eighteen grandchildren and four more on the way. In a sick way, it makes me happy to know I'm not the only disappointment to my parents on the grandchildren front (although I'm probably a disappointment on far more fronts than Joe is). Then I remind myself that for all I know, Joe could have five kids with six different baby mamas. He could have lied to me about everything.

Joe has one hundred seventy-two Facebook friends, zero in common with me. A lot of them are having babies, too. Is that why he's so interested in me? As a young and fit but anti-social woman, am I a prime target for rapid impregnation? Am I to be baby mama number seven? I shake the thought from my head. We've been on two dates; surely that's the furthest thing from his mind. It better be, anyway. Speaking of dates, his Facebook relationship status leaves some confusion. Of course, it reads "It's Complicated," but there are several pictures of him tagged with a girl named Felicia Blackwell. I switch back to the email app and search for emails from Felicia Blackwell, only to have the list populate before I can even finish typing.

I scroll through the subject lines—most of them are girlfriend-to-boyfriend type messages: CC-ing on dinner reservation confirmations, forwarded invitations for friends' engagement parties, flight itineraries, all signed "Hugs, F." The emails begin two years ago and end about a month ago, right around the time he started talking to me. Is that what this is about? Am I his no-basketball rebound girl? The girl who mysteriously dropped off the dodgeball team because she got too pregnant to take ball shots to the stomach—was it Felicia Blackwell? Was *she* baby mama number seven? I close out of the app to check today's date against the last email from Felicia, only to discover that two hours have gone by and I still haven't brushed the beer smell off my teeth. What would Dad think? And my car—I must get back to my car.

I take a deep breath and exit Room 403, leaving Joe's phone in there and shutting the door behind me. I check the class schedule at the community center in the catalog with my face on it. I can't let the previous evening's setback keep me from continuing down my path to some semblance of mental and social stability. I've only done one group class so far, and I know from experience that if I don't keep the streak going, if I break the chain, I'll fizzle out and find myself working out in a padded room where there's nothing to steal. On the plus side, at least I'll be able to attempt some more daring fitness feats that the fear of a hard floor keeps me from doing today. I shake the thought from my head. I can't think about that; I need to get my aching (but noticeably firmer feeling) ass to the gym. As an added plus, I know this is a time slot where Officer Joe is noticeably absent from it.

Because it's the next class on the schedule, I decide to try out the 2 p.m. F.I.T. group class. F.I.T. stands for Functional Integrated Training, and the description in the community center catalog seems innocuous enough. After yesterday's yoga, I now know not to arrive to these group classes too early, since I will inevitably end up just standing around awkwardly in a room full of people who see each other every week waiting for class to start. My heart rate's still up from the over two-mile walk I briskly took to get here for fear I would be late (and the McDouble and fries I picked up and ate along the way), but I decide to spend five of the ten minutes I have to spare before class starts on the treadmill anyway.

I enter the Jayhawks room to discover that this class requires a lot of accessories. I see what I can only assume are the class regulars preparing little equipment stations around them more meticulously than I've seen triathletes do. There appear to be three sets of weights for each person—heavy, medium, and light. Then there's a step with two risers, one to two yoga mats, and a couple resistance bands. Naturally, none of this equipment is in this room, so I now have five minutes to go get it from the stretching and free weights area and haul it all back in here. At least now I know where all the equipment mysteriously disappears to from time to time.

I finally get back from my third trip to get more equipment to find the obnoxiously muscular instructor giving high fives with one hand and adjusting the volume on his headset with the other.

"All right! Mission, Kansas how we doin'?!" he says in that overly enthusiastic fitness instructor voice that his kind are born with. He starts by rattling off the long list of equipment we'll need for the class, which sounds even more excessive than it looks. I nudge my ridiculous pile of gear closer to the wall I might as well already be hugging, so as to avoid getting kicked in the face by the girl in front of me, a front-row-er who has taken the equipment requirement to the extreme: four sets of weights and four risers under her step.

Some people think that the back row is where you go to hide, but anyone who's ever skated through high school without a teacher ever even noticing they were there will tell you otherwise. The best strategy is to hide in plain sight—particularly from a fitness instructor who wants you to "push just a *little* bit more"— you never go for either the center of the room or the back row. Always pick a blind spot. The front half of the room, far to one side or the other—this is where I can, and do, get away with stealing shit.

He prompts us to begin the warmup phase of the class, which puts me and the classmates who look far less awkward than me into a wide-legged, deep squat, bending at the torso to bring opposite elbows to our knees. My quads begin burning about twenty seconds in and I expect that any second now he's going to tell us to stand up and shake it out, but instead he shouts out "4, 3, 2, Double time, GO!" I feel yesterday's beer disagreeing with the command as it starts to churn its way up my esophagus. I swallow hard.

Just in case I've stumbled into an alternate universe where looks can kill, I shut my eyes as he keeps us in the squat but now instead of bringing alternating elbows to knees, we're bringing alternating hands to ankles. By now, my legs are shaking visibly and I can feel the famous burn they keep trying to convince me is the key to progress.

"All right! You guys are amazing! Now that we've warmed up, we're gonna kick it up a little."

Fuck me. Although kicking implies that we finally get to come out of this death squat. He instructs us to pick up the heavy weights, the orange ones for me. I can certainly go heavier, but I wasn't really sure what to expect and no one but the overachiever in the front row and the small population of guys in the class had anything heavier than an orange. He starts grinding us through a series of lifts that I've never seen done in my entire life, beginning with bicep lifts, then pulsing the lift right in the middle and rotating our wrists like we're turning a doorknob—two eight-pound doorknobs covered in cracked neoprene coating.

The feeling I had in my quads during the "warm up" has now migrated to my arms. The five-pound dumbbells in front of me look so inviting, but no one else is wussing out so I don't either (even though I'm in the blind spot and no one would ever notice).

"Okay, awesome people . . . drop the weights and grab your mats. It's time for Spartan pushups!" he says through a shit-eating grin and matching fitness instructor tone of voice that's supposed to trick us into thinking this is something to be excited about.

The smell of the community center's mats is even less inviting than the freshly unpackaged formaldehyde aroma of my yoga mat yesterday, and I try not to think of the number of sweaty asses that have been cushioned by this very mat, a short inch from my face. I make a mental note to always bring my own yoga mat to the gym, whether I end up needing it or not, just in case. Besides, the more I use it, the more I can justify the ludicrous amount I spent on all that gear.

I've attempted to do Spartan pushups as part of my circuit training, but I wouldn't say I've ever done them well. It's not particularly difficult—you just stagger one arm in front of the other instead of keeping them square—but it feels incredibly awkward. At this moment, however, I'm doing them more poorly than I ever have because my arms are so spaghetti-y I can barely even hold myself up in high plank position. The last time I did a girl push up was one of the few times I "remembered" my gym clothes in high school, but I know if I attempt to do a regular-ass pushup now, I will only collapse and faceplant into the yoga mat, so I relent and drop my knees to the edge of my sweat-embedded mat.

"You guys are SO good! Now we're going to ex-PLODE through our arms and switch Spartan hand positions on our mats. It's gonna be amazing!"

I couldn't explode through my arms right now if someone chopped off my legs and I had to crawl through fire to survive. The only thing exploding out of me right now is my breath (I'd say last night's pasta, but I seem to have gotten all that out of my system in yoga) and possibly a blood vessel in my right eyeball. I focus on my watch to keep last night's beer from exploding out of me and see that we're only fifteen minutes into a one-hour class. The building could always spontaneously collapse, right? I attempt to look up toward the ceiling rafters to see if there's any possibility of this happening but instead all I see is the perfectly toned ass of the overachiever in front of me, exploding through her Spartan pushups like it's the easiest thing in the world. Where's the Unabomber when I need him?

"If you want a little more challenge," he begins. *No, thanks.* "Just take your arms out wide." *Increasing your risk of breaking your own nose by a mere 2000 percent.*

To get myself through what may not be the most excruciating hour of my life but is certainly up there, I let my eyes wander as we repeat the arm torture on our legs. As movements become sloppier and sloppier the more we extend then pulse the muscle groups in our legs I was not familiar with before today, steps begin sliding out from under people and I see that the space between the risers and the step is clearly the hiding spot of choice for most of the class's belongings.

Not that I'm counting, but it's been seven days since I've stolen anything from someone—an impressive streak that I've only matched a couple times in my life, and one of them was when I had swine flu. A purple pair of earbuds catches my eye. It's the exact shade of purple I wanted to paint my room when I was a kid but my parents wouldn't let me because they said it was too dark. It may not be healthy, but I now have another motivator for getting through this class, so I can find a way to swipe these earbuds that I've decided absolutely must be mine. I've had a very long twenty-four hours already and I need something to calm my nerves. Definitely something non-alcoholic this time.

"How are our legs feeling? Do we need more?!" *No.*

"Yeah!" comes a shout from right in front of me. I'm not the only one who shoots the brunette in Lululemons a death stare.

"All right! You asked for it!" *Well,* I *didn't. Can I get a pass?*

The music slows to a still very much up-tempo version of "I

Believe I Can Fly" and I hope the instructor has a better under-
standing of cool down than he has of warmup. The only thing I
believe I can do right now is stop for a pint of Orange Dreamsicle
ice cream on the way home, but I move through the cool down
exercises anyway, glancing at my watch every ten seconds to see
if he's going to dismiss us on time.

As he over-enthusiastically dismisses us from class with a
"can't wait to see you all next week!" (fat chance), I collapse on
my back on a mat, waiting for my breathing to return to a normal
pace. I no longer care whose ass has been on it. The owner of the
purple earbuds is none other than the tiny brunette in the Lululemons who wanted the extra round of leg work. Clearly the
universe has picked me to tip the scales of justice in everyone's
favor by relieving her of her headphones.

As the classroom turns into a swarm of people collecting
their accessories and a select few heading out to put them away, I
easily snatch the earbuds on my way to the weight rack. I have to
make a trip back for the step and the risers, at which time I notice
two things. One, a little less than half of the people from class
have abandoned their gear with no intention of putting it away
in its proper place, like a pack of goddamned animals. Two, the
leggy brunette is searching for her now-missing earbuds, bending
over in her Lululemon pants that do little to hide the fact that
she's wearing a thong. What kind of alien monster does Spartan
pushups in a thong?

I should just turn around and walk out, but it makes me too
angry to see all this equipment left lying about like it's someone
else's job to clean it up, and if I'm being honest, it's making me
feel wickedly content watching this girl get all flustered. I casually begin piling up as much equipment as I can carry (which
isn't much in my state with my muscles now feeling like shredded cheese) and hauling it to the other room, trip after trip, until

the only people left in the Jayhawks room are the brunette, the instructor, and myself.

"Something wrong?" he asks, trading his overly enthusiastic fitness instructor voice for a masculine damsel-in-distress-rescuing voice.

"I coulda sworn I brought my earbuds in but now I can't find them! They were *right here*," she seethes, pointing to the spot previously occupied by her step.

"Maybe someone will turn them into the lost and found," he says.

She lets out an exasperated sigh and storms out. I pick up the last of the figure-eight bands and attempt to make a hasty exit when I am intercepted by the instructor. I gasp audibly.

"Hey, thanks for your help! You didn't have to clean up after all these jerks," the overly enthusiastic voice says back.

I force a smile. "Don't mention it. Someone's gotta do it, right?"

"You KILLED it out there!" he exclaims, raising a signature high-five hand. The only thing I killed tonight was a little bit of my will to live, and perhaps a certain brunette's spirit. Still, it's rude to leave a high five hanging, so I lift a very shaky arm and muster the best slap I can, my arms immediately reminding me of the two days of torture I've now put them through. I don't care what time it is; after ice cream, I'm going straight to bed.

Before I can exit the gym, I feel my phone vibrate through my bag and pull it out. It's a text message.

"How r u feeling today? Need me 2 take u back 2 ur car?"

Joe. He already had my phone number and now he knows where I live, too. I wince at the phone and type out a quick one-word response.

"No."

I better be one sexy-looking bitch tomorrow.

Chapter 21

☺"FELICIA"☺

I drive home, thankful that I was able to avoid running into Average Joe and that my car Rosa was waiting for me in the parking lot without so much as a brightly-colored warning about parking overnight on city property. My legs are so weak my left calf quivers as I ease off the clutch between gears. Climbing the stairs to my apartment, every muscle in my body emits silent Godzilla screams, reinforcing the conviction that I'm never drinking beer again, and that F.I.T. is clearly not the class for me. No one should have to be that hardcore. Key in the lock, breathing heavily from exhaustion and the trip up the stairs, I catch a whiff of myself, an overwhelmingly unpleasant mix of body odor laced with day-old beer. My stomach turns as I struggle to enter my apartment.

Making a beeline for the shower, I peel off my clothes not caring where they fall along the way. I get all the way to the bathroom before I realize I'm still holding the earbuds I stole from Lulu Lemonade. I drop them and jump back as if I've been holding a hot coal this whole time, but quickly decide to push them aside for now. My brain, much like the rest of my body, has been reduced to mush and doesn't have enough functioning cells to process any next actions besides washing the F.I.T. and beer stank off me.

The blasting water beats against my body, massaging my aching muscles back to life. I try not to think about the earbuds, but it's like my brain won't let any other thoughts in. Was taking them any different from taking any of the countless other things that sit in Room 403, piled up on the other side of the wall I'm leaning against for support? Although I can barely lift my arms overhead, I dig my fingers into my scalp, using shampoo as a catalyst to inspire higher brain function.

For whatever reason, it works, and I come to realize that the earbud theft feels a little bit different. I didn't steal them because I had a compulsion to do so; I stole them to deliberately hurt someone. Maybe it's not any healthier for my social sanity to see the other person as an object of hatred (as opposed to not seeing her as a person at all), but then, maybe it is. Maybe Dr. Kelley was right about this whole group class thing. If nothing else, she was definitely right about it giving me a firmer butt—between F.I.T. and yoga, I'm walking like an ass-raped clown on stilts.

I exit the shower and haphazardly wrap a towel around my body as I head straight for Room 403, dripping even more water onto the bathroom tile as I realize I forgot to close the shower curtain in my brain's temporary myopic state. I take a deep breath before opening the door. As I let the scene before me sink in, I think of all the things I could do with this room if it wasn't full of all this crap I didn't need in the first place that just sits here collecting dust and reminding me of my own failures. I think of all the things in here I could actually use if they weren't sitting buried under more things. The room is so quiet I can hear my phone buzzing next to the bathroom sink. I better get it before it vibrates itself off the counter and crashes into a pool of water below.

It's my mother. I don't answer and let it go to voice mail. I make a half-hearted attempt to dry myself off as I wait for the voice mail notification to pop up. I throw on a pair of happy pants and a t-shirt thin enough that I can justify wearing Joe's cardigan over it, shoving my phone into its pocket just as the voicemail chime goes off.

"Ann, this is your mother. I know you're just going to listen to this voicemail as soon as I hang up instead of talking to me, but I forgive you for it. Don't forget that we have dinner reservations tonight at Story in downtown Prairie Village at 6:30. Be a lamb and try not to be late; your father has surgery in the morning. Love you, bye."

I roll my eyes. Only my mother could make molar extraction sound like a craniotomy, and make it sound like my dad were the one having surgery, not performing it. I had completely forgotten about dinner. Was it really next month already? I briefly wonder if all my monthly bills are paid and start to check my flimsy financial accounting records, but quickly abandon it and return my focus to the task at hand—beginning the daunting process of organizing the contents of Room 403. My phone chimes another voice mail, but again I decide not to check it. It's probably just Mom relaying an absurd detail about dinner that she neglected to mention in her first passive-aggressive voice mail in order to leave another passive-aggressive voice mail, and I don't need the distraction. I turn off my phone so I won't obsessively check the time every five minutes.

I start by dividing the room into four sections: wearables, gadgets, fitness equipment, and everything else. Before I know it, I turn my phone back on and it's 4:30. Two hours have gone by, and the one mountainous pile of stuff in the middle becomes four disparate piles retreating to the corners of the otherwise empty but very dingy room. I glance at my phone, where I am again reminded of the voice mail I haven't listened to yet, and see that I still have another two hours until dinner with the parents. I feel like I should keep going and turn my phone back off. I drag out the vacuum that needs to be vacuumed itself and run it over the floor of Room 403 for the first time since the last Bush administration.

From there, I further divide each of the four piles into things I will use and things I won't. I'm alarmed by the number of duplicate items I've amassed over the years, and am simultaneously transported back to the moments I remember taking the items. Some of them, anyway. Most of this shit I have no memory of taking whatsoever. "Compulsion has little connection with feeling or memory," Dr. Kelley is fond of saying. I save the wearables pile for last. With the exception of Joe's cardigan (which I never wear in public) and a few dime-a-dozen staple apparel items, I've never worn anything out of this room once I transported it back here, for fear someone would recognize his or her clothing on a stranger's body. It's a ridiculous notion now that I think about it. I rarely even pay attention to what *I* am wearing, and only notice it on other people because it's the only way I interact. Are normal people really perceptive enough to notice what other people wear?

Besides, I remind myself, most of the clothes in this pile are just factory made, mass manufactured bits of polyester. Still, I keep the "things I'll use" portion of the pile small, partially because of the growing fear of getting caught wearing someone else's clothes and partially because it's mostly stuff I legitimately would never wear. My mother donates the better part of her entire closet to the Junior League thrift store every year; I wonder if she ever notices someone on the street wearing something that used to belong to her. Probably not—she's likely consumed enough red zinfandel by now that all memories of past season's wardrobes have faded into oblivion.

One cute top in particular catches my eye. At the time, I probably didn't think it was something I would wear (I have no memory of taking it no matter how hard I try to remember), but as I hold it up the light, I see that apart from the deep wrinkles caused by sitting in a ball for who knows how long, it'd be very flattering on me. I shake it out as I make my way to the bathroom, where the floor has finally dried, and try it on in front of the mirror. It looks great on me, and part of me wishes I'd stuffed this shirt into my gym bag yesterday for my second date with Joe instead of the stupid dentist conference freebie. I check the label—H&M—plenty of people buy cheap, mass-produced couture at H&M. No one would immediately identify it as theirs if I wore it to dinner tonight, just to run a test.

I decide that I've made enough progress on Room 403 for one day and don't even realize that a wide smile has spread across my face until I catch my reflection in the mirror, still wearing the cute but wrinkled top. The only thing still sitting in the middle of the room is Joe's iPhone, playing Joe's music for me where I left it this morning after my too-long snooping session. I had no idea Alice in Chains had so many albums. We have different tastes. Looking at it, I remember that I have an unread voice mail still waiting for me on my own phone.

I turn it back on and acknowledge the notification, and up pops a local number from the Missouri side that I don't recognize. Definitely not my mother—she doesn't even acknowledge that the other half of Kansas City that lies in another state exists, let alone venture there and make a phone call. I press play.

"Hey Ann, it's Joe. I just wanted to check in and see how you were feeling today. I was patrolling earlier and saw that you came and got your car at some point, so you must still be alive, which makes me happy."

There is an awkward silence and I can practically hear him thinking of what to say next.

"Sorry last night got weird or whatever. Anyway, call me back when you get a chance, or I'll see you at the community center soon. Just call, okay?"

The line clicks off and my phone asks me if I want to replay the message or delete it. I want to replay it over and over again, read way too much into every voice inflection and awkward pause, but I decide it would be better for my burgeoning sanity to just delete it. If I indulge my desires, I'll be late for dinner, and my mother wants me to "be a lamb." I keep wondering where he called me from—an interrogation room at the police station littered with cold case files?

Out of curiosity, though, I unlock Joe's iPhone and go to his voice mail app. He has seven new voice mails. I feel a lump rise in my throat as the play button taunts me. There's still so much to explore on this phone, but I can't help but feel guilty just hovering over the voice mails from "Tina Willis (Mom)," "Pops," "The Chief," "Chad," (who I assume is one of his four brothers), and finally, at the bottom of the list, "☺Felicia☺," which must be the same Felicia Blackwell from the emails. Happy faces? What's that about? Did she program her own number into his phone, maybe? Joe hardly strikes me as an emoji person, but then I didn't expect him to get sports notifications on his phone either, based on our earlier conversations. Or be a cop. I have to accept that everything I know about him has a big fat question mark behind it.

I push the play button on the voice mail from ☺Felicia☺ and put the phone to my ear. The message starts with an exasperated sigh before she starts speaking. Her voice is simultaneously dusty and chirpy.

"Hey, Joe. I know it's been a while but I heard about your grandpa and wanted to make sure you're doing okay. But, you know, you haven't been returning my calls and I haven't run into you. I just want to make sure you're okay. So, you know, call me. Bye."

I push replay and start to bring the phone up to my ear, but instead, I hurl it at the wall with all the force I can muster from my very, very sore shoulder. The phone bounces off the wall and the carpet but the screen goes dead. I pick it up and launch it at the wall over and over until it shatters into tiny pieces across the clean stuff room floor. I can't process this right now.

Chapter 22

BLOUSE

My mother scowls at me over the rim of her chardonnay spritzer when I order chicken strips and fries, a kid's menu item that for some reason costs thirteen dollars.

"Dr. Kelley says you've been going to all of your sessions."

I'm not sure if I'm supposed to say anything, confirmation-wise or not, so I just nod.

"Well," she says, leaning forward as if we're having a secret mother-to-daughter talk, not a scheduled meal in a bourgeois suburban restaurant. "How's it going?"

"Dr. Kelley hasn't told you?" I ask.

"No," she scowls, leaning back in her plush upholstered chair. "She won't tell us anything about your progress no matter how much we ask. Says it's doctor–patient confidentiality."

"Even though we're the ones footin' the bill," my father chimes in, the first thing he's said since I got here besides "It's about time; I'm starving."

"It's going well," I say, trying to decide how honest to be, always a debate when talking to my parents. "I'm following her plan and it seems to be making a real difference."

"We're so glad to hear that." My chicken strips and whatever overpriced entrées my parents ordered arrive. "We appreciate that you're honoring our agreement, don't we, Bill?"

Dad grunts in huffy agreement, violently shaking salt onto his plate. I notice my mother shift her disapproving eyeballs from me to Dad.

"I must say, Ann," she says, returning her eyes to me, "that blouse is quite striking on you."

I've never liked the word *blouse*. It sounds like something worn by people in their nineties, not their twenties. Gladyses wear blouses.

"Thanks," I say without making eye contact, alternating dipping my chicken strips and fries into ranch dressing.

"Where'd you get it?" she asks.

"J Crew," I say. It's the first thing that comes into my head. I have no idea why, or why I lied about it. Then again, we are in the J Crewiest corner of the city; could be I drove by at least one on my way in.

"Well, it's lovely. You should definitely wear it the next time you go out with that boy you've been seeing," she says with a smirk, picking apart her tilapia with her fork.

"What?"

"Mrs. Schultz from Junior League told me she saw you on a date with this nice boy, a police officer, from the community center. I have to admit I was so taken aback I told Mrs. Schultz that she must have been mistaken, but she was just adamant and told me she was positive it was you."

I try not to show that I'm swallowing a giant lump in my throat around the chicken strip batter, a little salty for my taste. Dad would love it. How in the world does my mom know what

Joe does for a living without ever having met him, but it took me two for-real dates to figure it out? And who the hell is Mrs. Schultz and how does she know? And who refers to a grown man—a police officer—as a "nice boy"? I open my mouth to ask this when I feel a hand on my shoulder and jump in shock instead. I turn to see a soccer mom stranger smiling down at me like we're old friends.

"Excuse me, I didn't mean to scare you; I just couldn't help but notice your top. I used to have the exact same one. Got it at H&M."

"Couldn't be," my mother interrupts. "That blouse is J Crew."

"No, no way. I'd remember that. I got it at H&M and then one day when I was at the gym, someone took it right out of my locker. Can you believe that? I went back to the store to get another one but they didn't stock them anymore. I was so disappointed. What kind of person steals someone's clothes? At the gym, no less?"

"Ann, you said you got it from J Crew," Mom says. I attempt to smile but even though I can't see it, I can tell it's probably a frightening sight.

"I—I must've forgotten. Maybe I got it from a thrift store," I say, instantly regretting it.

"A thrift store? Really?" the soccer mom with the blonde bob squeals. "Could you tell me which one? Maybe they have more." Clearly, she has no idea how thrift store inventory works.

"Ann, what are you doing shopping at a thrift store? Is it the Junior League one, at least? Is money that tight for you?" my mother says, nearly choking on the remainder of her spritzer. "Bill, I *told* you!" she attempts to say under her boozy breath but it comes out at normal volume.

"I'm sorry," I say, feeling like all of the words flying around me are collecting in my lap and my chair might collapse under me at any moment from the weight of it. I shoot up out of my chair; both my mother and the stranger jump a little in surprise. Dad is still too focused on his T-bone to notice.

"I have to go use the ladies' room. I'm sorry; I don't think I remember where I got the shirt. It was a long time ago."

"Well, shoot. I knew it was a long shot but I just liked that top so much I figured it couldn't hurt to ask. Enjoy the rest of your meal. So sorry to bother you," the woman says with a polite half-curtsy.

I turn and near-jog to the bathroom, locking the door behind me and catching my reflection in the posh, vintage-framed mirror. My face is red with shame and I hadn't even noticed I was wringing my hands, pulling at the tips of my fingers one by one. I immediately go to shove my hands in my pockets only to discover that the black dress pants I chose to pair with the H&M top (the conversation piece of the evening) don't have real pockets, only fake ones.

I have to get out of this top. The one time I decide to make use out of something I stole and I have to look into the face of the previously unknown person I stole it from. I didn't even bring a jacket to wear over it because I wanted to look good in my flashy top. Now I remember why I don't dress up, why I try to blend in and hope no one ever notices me. Lately I've had too many people noticing me and I can't handle it. I need to go home and stay there with my room full of things that used to make me feel safe. I never feel safe anymore, not even in Room 403.

But first, I need to figure out a way to finish my dinner with my parents. Maybe I can invent seeing a cockroach here in the bathroom and tell Mom all about it.

Chapter 23

CRD

I call Dr. Kelley's office first thing the next day. After she chastises me for calling and demanding answers instead of making an appointment like a normal client, she says the only way I can overcome the kind of mania I experienced yesterday is to "keep stepping out of my comfort zone and trying new things to foster growth." She also insists that this means continuing my epic group class journey at the community center. For posterity, I suppose, she doesn't let me hang up until I do make an official appointment with her for tomorrow.

Despite the fact that I suffer from CRD (Caucasian Rhythmic Disorder, also known colloquially as "white girl can't dance"), the Shake and Sweat cardio dance class on tonight's group class calendar looks like it is potentially the most fun, and after the collective disasters of yoga and F.I.T., I feel like I could use a little fun. I even wear the sexiest of my vast super-tight fitness pants repertoire and my flame red sports bra to get myself into the spirit.

Thankfully, Shake and Sweat takes place in the Chiefs room, and not on the open gym floor where all the soccer moms pushing strollers around the track can point and laugh at me. Not that it really matters, because it appears all the soccer moms have left their strollers behind for the evening and are in here for class anyway. No wonder the track is so sparsely populated on Tuesdays; I make note of this for future reference.

Apparently, everyone in this room is fantastic friends with someone else except for me, because they're all hugging one another and catching up on their kids' progress in potty training. The only one not talking about potty training (besides myself) is the incredibly flamboyant gay male in cosmic cat apparel occupying the middle-center of the room, but that's only because he's too busy hugging everyone in the room as if they're all old BFFs. Or is it BFsF? Either way, I never would have thought soccer moms to be such fruit flies.

I position myself where I think I'll be able to hide but still see the instructor, who has not yet made an appearance, behind a curvy yoga-pants-and-skirt clad soccer mom with a perfect ponytail who looks like she knows the ropes of Shake and Sweat. If nothing else, she seems to know everyone else here, so clearly, she's been here more times than me. Class is supposed to start in eight minutes, and because I have no one to hug or talk toddler wisdom with, and would prefer to not stand around sticking out like a sore thumb for the entire interval, I sit down to stretch the same muscles I already stretched in the main gym area.

A teeny-tiny woman in a headset, skin-tight floral print spandex pants, and a hot pink tank top that reads SWEATING FOR TWO strides up to the front of the room and it's all I can do to suppress an eyeroll. On the plus side, though, maybe she'll go a little easier on us given that she's with child. She fumbles with the headset controls and clips them to her spandex pants before greeting the class in a chirpy voice.

"Haaaaaaay y'all! Welcome to Shake and Sweat! How we all doin' on this Tuesday night?"

A cacophony of whoops and hollers emanates from the crowd of soccer moms, and spirit fingers go up from the gay guy. Now I remember the other reason I avoided group activities—the relentless stream of unsubstantiated enthusiasm from the fake, overly exuberant voice of the instructor. She chirps at us again, this time in a voice even more annoyingly zealous.

"Is this anyone's first time to Shake and Sweat?"

Before I can even think about what I am doing, my hand instinctively shoots up and I suddenly realize that not only is everyone else in the room staring at me, but the only hand up in the room is mine.

"Terrific! Well, remember, the first and foremost thing to Shake and Sweat is to have fun. You should have no problems keeping up, but if at any time you get lost, *this* is totally acceptable." She demonstrates *this* by tapping alternating feet to the rhythm of the will.I.am and Justin Bieber song she just queued up. *I got that power.*

"All right, let's warm up!"

We start stepping from side to side, adding claps after the first count of eight, the highest number to which cardio instructors can count. Then instead of stepping, we're squatting and rotating our hips first to the right, then the left. I immediately realize that I am far more adept at doing everything to the right, and doing anything to the left requires brain power that I currently need to keep up with the instructor. For her part, she is in the most impressive squat I have ever seen, one that makes my thighs hurt just looking at it, shaking the hips under her little baby bump so vigorously that I bet the fetus is getting a workout by osmosis.

Before I even realize we've come out of the shaky squats, I see everyone in the class spinning around to the right. All I can do is stand there frozen in shock as the person immediately to my left nearly crashes into me. I then attempt to catch up as we repeat the motion to the left, but my left turn leaves much to be desired and I nearly trip over my own feet. We repeat the spin pattern, and I sort of hit it moving to the right, although I'm pretty sure I led with the wrong foot.

I desperately continue to try and keep up, finally figuring out each move just in time for the instructor to squawk "Now add the arms!" or "To the left!" and get me lost all over again. The percentage of people in class putting me to shame is 100 percent, with special emphasis on the curvy soccer mom in front of me with the perfect ponytail, the brightly-clad and overly enthusiastic instructor (who exhibits more sex appeal and energy visibly pregnant than I do), and the gay guy, who is absolutely killing it. As we shimmy back and forth and pump our arms to "Sexy-Back," the instructor takes the opportunity to call him out on his vigorous shimmying ability.

"This ain't HIS first rodeo!"

Another round of cheers comes up from the crowd and the gay guy is now the center of attention, shimmying with an extra shake of the hips and loving it. *He got his sexy out.* How anyone can be that comfortable with himself with that many eyes focused in his direction is beyond me. I glance at my watch between shimmies and feel my heart sink as I realize there are still forty long minutes left in class.

The only time anyone else begins to match my level of lost is when the instructor adds a new move—two pumps forward, two pumps back, and instead does the opposite, which she dismisses by saying "This prego brain, I tell ya!"

She then takes a poll about how people prefer to end class, either with a slow jam cool down or with Rihanna, which clearly implies the opposite of a slow jam cool down without any further explanation. The class responds with a resounding cheer to Rihanna over cool down, which makes me groan out loud (not that anyone can hear me over the music). *It better not be the same Rihanna mix they use every time in step aerobics.* I already know I'm not the only girl in the world, but I admit I am curious to see how the gay guy responds to this challenge. Thankfully, it's a different song—and a newer one—and the guy does not fail to disappoint. At least I have one source of entertainment besides reflecting on my own ineptitude.

Class ends with a session of rhythmic clapping and I struggle to match the beat of the music as opposed to the beat of my racing heart. It's hard for me to believe I could get my heart rate up that high with how much of class I spent hopelessly flailing my arms and reversing course with my feet, but apparently, I somehow managed it because my chest is heaving rapidly. Not burpee-rapidly, but definitely respectable-rapidly.

I dart out quickly, not wanting to watch as everyone high fives one another and repeats the same hugging ritual they already did only an hour ago. Across from the Chiefs room is the small row of even smaller lockers people never lock. There were so many people in Shake and Sweat class that most of the belongings are stuffed into monogrammed diaper bags in a pile below the lockers. I do a quick scan with my eyes; I certainly have no use for a diaper bag, but I will take a neon yellow yoga mat, which I grab and stuff under my right arm before heading down the stairs.

A voice from behind stops me.

"Hey, sweaty." I turn around; it's Joe. *Cue heavy sinking feeling. Play it cool.*

"Um . . . excuse me?"

"Wow. I'm sorry. I saw you in Shake and Sweat. I thought about saying 'hey, shaky' but somehow 'hey, sweaty' sounded better. Now that I said it, I realize it doesn't. Let me try again."

He turns around and scales a couple of stairs before turning around and coming back down the same two steps. He's blushing. I've never seen him blush before and it's insanely cute.

"Hey, beautiful."

I can't help but smile, and hope my grin doesn't look as confused as I feel. "Hey. You were watching me?"

"No, not really," he says, starting to blush again. "I just—saw you? I didn't think Shake and Sweat was your kinda thing but it looked like you were having fun in there."

Oh God, I think to myself. I hope that between the low lighting in the room and the small window people can use to see in, I looked less inept than I really was. How long had he been watching me? Why did he even look in there in the first place, especially if he thought it wasn't my kind of thing? Does he always do a lecherous once-over for Shake and Sweat?

"It's not my thing. And I wasn't having fun. In fact, I'm never doing that again," I say, still struggling to catch my breath.

He laughs, and I see the muscles in his chest rising and falling. "Well, I had fun the other night. Let me know when you'd like to do it again. The dodgeball is completely in your court."

For a minute, I wonder if he's remembering the same evening that I remember. Did I get so drunk that I blacked out and had a wonderful time? No, that couldn't be it; he wouldn't have left me that message the next day.

"Dodgeball?" I say.

"Of course," he says, flashing his brilliant smile again. I

wonder if it's the same smile he used for Felicia. "You're still on our team, right?"

I start to remind him about how badly I embarrassed myself on our last post-dodgeball outing, but from the way he's talking, I guess we're not going there, so I don't go there.

"Yes. Of course. I'll be there. Thursday night, right?"

Chapter 24

BAG LADY

"So," Dr. Kelley says once she finally enters the cramped consultation room I've been awkwardly waiting in for fifteen minutes. "You wanna tell me how things are going?"

I straighten myself with a deep breath and proceed to tell her about the incident at dinner with my parents, right down to the detail about the chicken strips and the lace trim on the stolen shirt from the mythical land of H&M. She listens to my stream of consciousness word vomit for several minutes before she cuts me off.

"I don't mean how did it go at dinner," she says. "Tell me how it's going with your group classes at the community center."

"Oh," I say, somewhat taken aback. I expected her to ask about my thoughts and feelings, and my parents, since they're the ones footing the bill for my therapy sessions. "I don't know. I haven't really found a class that's *me*. All the classes I've gone to so far feel like they've been a disaster. I just wanna go back to the solo rotation I had before."

"Because you feel like you're not getting the physical results you want from the classes, or because they make you feel socially uncomfortable?" she asks.

I shrug. I don't have to tell her that it's the latter. She already knows.

"You can't expect to move forward if all you're willing to do is step back," she says, glancing at her watch. It could be one of the framed motivational posters on the walls of the community center. "Listen, I was only able to squeeze you in for a short time, but because you called I really wanted you to come in, so I'm going to get straight to the point, okay?"

I nod.

"Maybe you'll find a class you enjoy, and maybe you won't," she says, drawing symmetrical boxes on her legal pad again. She continues without looking up.

"That's not the point. The point is to get you interacting with others in an environment that works for you. From everything I'm observing based on what you're telling me, it's working. It may not seem like it to you because all these uncomfortable moments are happening now that you've started this journey, but that's what progress looks like." She pauses for an uncomfortable amount of time before her eyes dart up to meet mine.

"But . . ." I start to say something close to the truth but it won't come out.

"Your sociopathy is diminishing; you're just too close to it to see it."

She pauses, staring directly at me with an expectant look on her face. I avert my eyes but it eventually gets so awkward I take my cue to say something.

"So, I'm getting better?" I ask.

"You are."

"But—" I start, trying to force the next words out. "I made

categorized piles of things. I rummaged through Joe's iPhone and invaded his personal life. I threw the phone at a wall until it exploded. I got trashed and had to have him drive me home. I wore a shirt I stole from someone out to dinner with my parents. I created a replica of a day planner I stole from one of the community center workers. I even ran it over with my car!"

I pause, trying to determine from her facial expression whether I should continue. There's plenty more unhealthy behavior where that came from; I can keep going.

"And all those things are part of becoming the new Ann. The old Ann would just keep taking things from people at the gym and think nothing of it." She stands, again glancing impatiently at her watch.

"Don't go," I say, surprised at how petulant the voice that escapes me sounds.

"I have to go. I have another patient who needs me more than you do right now. What you need to do is find another group class to attend today. Call my office tomorrow and tell me how it goes."

"But what if I steal something again?" I say at her back.

She turns, opening the door and holding it open. "Then it will have happened and you'll have to process the feelings from that and deal with the consequences. But I don't think you will."

I don't take her up on her unspoken invitation to leave through the open door.

"You can see yourself out," she says. "Oh, and I know you don't care, but tell your father I won't be charging him for this session."

Once I get home, I look through the paper catalog I wish I could collect every copy of and burn. I rabidly flip past all the educational classes on tax preparation, English as a second language, and Irish pennywhistle, though I do pause to see that its instruc-tor believes it is "the most versatile instrument in the musical universe." I've never personally felt a strong desire to learn to play a music instrument, but I have a feeling this instructor, whoever he or she is, could be my soulmate based on this class description alone.

I continue flipping the pages until I finally reach the fitness section. I dog-ear the first page, something I should have done a long time ago, and give myself a mental pat on the back for saving my future self valuable time. That's something a normal person would do, right? The classes tonight are: Senior Aqua-robics (with the Gladyses—pass), Zumba (a more Latin version of Shake and Sweat, been there done that—pass), Spinning (bike for an hour and see nothing—pass), and Cardio Kickboxing. The instructor's name is Lil and the class is in the Royals room, which is my favorite of the community center's selection of group fitness rooms. Not only is it quieter and more secluded from the rest of the gym, it's also the only one that the taxpay-er-supplied central air system operates in with any degree of reliability. Hopefully it's also a room where Officer Joe doesn't go a'leching.

I look at my heart rate monitor watch; cardio kickboxing class doesn't start for another three hours and there's nothing earlier that piques my interest. What am I going to do with myself for three whole hours? I feel like the kid who wakes up at 5 a.m. on Christmas morning knowing full well Mom and Dad won't wake up 'til eight. I could get some freelance work done; I'm already grossly behind where I need to be according to the timeline I pulled out of my ass and gave them at the start of this project, but my eyes aren't looking longingly at my overpriced Thunderbolt monitor. They're looking at the closed door to Room 403, where I still have some odds and ends left to classify into piles.

I make a deal with myself: I'll work for an hour then work in Room 403 for an hour. Or maybe I'll work in the stuff room for an hour and *then* get some project work done. For some reason, the latter makes more sense and I head to Room 403, taking a deep breath before opening the door. The first thing I see is the detritus of what was Joe's iPhone, highlighted by the afternoon sunlight pouring in through the dirty window. I simultaneously feel my heart sink and a lump rise in my throat. I remind myself that I did the right thing by destroying it and not continuing to pry further into his professional and personal life. I already know too much about his inane Johnson County investigations and ☺Felicia☺, who I believe to be his former flame. Does that make me his current flame? I *do* have that flame red sports bra I wore to Shake and Sweat . . .

I start by grabbing the already overflowing trash can from the kitchen and dragging it into Room 403, picking up the broken bits of iPhone that litter the floor and depositing them into the crevices of the trash bag where they won't fall back to the floor. I remove the full trash bag and procure a new one; I am purging after all, and I again praise myself for being so practical and efficient. This praise is short-lived as I rise from changing the trash bag and survey the room before me, seeing the forest through the trees now that the iPhone shards are out of the way.

What am I supposed to do with all this stuff? Why did I ever think taking it was a good idea? A wave of guilt and shame washes over me as I approach the "miscellaneous" pile and collapse into child's pose so I don't have to look at it. It's not like I can just return all this stuff, turn an entire room's worth of things into the lost and found bin little by little; it would take years and someone would figure me out. I could donate it all to charity, but last I checked Robin Hood didn't steal leggings from the middle class to give to the lower middle class. I could throw it all away, just toss it all into trash bags and put it out of my mind forever. It's not like I'm going to use any of these things, especially after my immediate karmic comeuppance with the pretty H&M blouse. Ugh, blouse. I hate that word so much.

If I throw it all away, will the garbageman somehow know that it all came from my apartment and turn me in to my new "flame," Average Joe? I could throw it away little by little, but if I do that, I run the risk of losing inertia after a week and second guessing myself. Who knows? One day I might need that GoPro headband for the GoPro I don't own, right? If I throw it all away now, the garbageman won't come until Friday. That's two whole days from now. Will I start dumpster diving tomorrow night after the full realization of what I've done punches me in my stupid face? Will the Catholic guilt I was baptized with eat at me from the inside for the sin of wastefulness?

I move my body into the seated meditation pose I learned in yoga and start visualizing like I do in my counseling sessions. I try to shut out all external stimuli, which really only consists of the humming of the fridge and the sun shining in blazing hot through the West window. I visualize myself returning everything to the community center, all at once and with penance to Remy the security guard, turning myself in and throwing myself on the mercy of Percival O'Shaughnessy himself. I then visualize myself sneaking little bits of things into the lost and found every day for the next three years, people walking right by the iPad sitting ostentatiously in the bin and not taking notice, but this proves more a difficult series of images to imagine.

I visualize hauling a boxed roomful of things to the Goodwill on the other side of State Line—surely I can't donate them to the Goodwill on Johnson drive; there's too much possibility of a JoCo mom finding her own Moby wrap (which at one point

I thought I could use as an indoor hammock) at the Goodwill two blocks away from where it was stolen. I visualize driving all the way out to Independence. Do they have iPads in Methdependence or would someone just steal the iPads to go trade for meth? *I know, I know,* I tell myself, *not everyone in IndepMo is a meth head.*

Finally, I visualize throwing it all away. If I throw it all away at once, maybe they'll just assume someone is moving out of his apartment and not think twice of it. We don't have a dumpster big enough for all this crap. I visualize bagging it all up and throwing it away two bags at a time week after week, stretching out the self-congratulatory gesture of freedom from the tyranny that is Room 403. Once everything is gone from here, I imagine turning the empty room into an office, putting my desk in here instead of in the kitchen/dining room and getting work done at regular intervals, taking on more clients, earning more money, making a name for myself.

I open my eyes and exhale. Since I feel better after this last visualization, I decide that's what I'll do. But first, I need to bag everything up so that I don't know what's in what bag and I won't give myself the opportunity to rip them open to retrieve one random item I feel like I can't do without based on the day's whim. I grab the roll of black trash sacks and furiously begin stuffing. With each one I fill up, I feel a little freer, a little lighter. Halfway through the room piles, the roll runs out and I start to panic. I still have two more big piles to go. I look at my watch; two hours have gone by and I don't have time to get any work done now. Maybe I should skip cardio kickboxing and go to the store right now for more trash bags, before I lose this bag lady inertia.

No, the counselor says go to class, so I need to go to class. I can stop by the store on the way home from the gym and finish up as soon as I get home. Then I can squeeze in an hour's worth of work before bed. No time lost, no responsibility shirked. Everything will be okay. I should definitely forgo the flame red sports bra tonight; it still reeks from Shake and Sweat and it didn't do me any favors. No sense bringing that same kind of karma into Cardio Kickboxing.

Chapter 25

NARCISSUS

I toss two bags in the dumpster on my way out to the gym. *Two bags at a time; slowly but surely,* I silently say to myself while swinging an overstuffed bag over the rim with a grunt that Gunther would be proud of. It lands with an echoing thud.

When I get to the community center, I enter the Royals room with the same kind of confidence I typically reserve only when stealing things, trying to convey that I belong to this class, that this ain't my first rodeo (like the Shake & Sweat instructor said), despite the fact that it is. I pick an open spot at the far-left front corner of the room, staring at myself in the mirror but still able to easily spot the instructor. I look around as I stretch my arms; no one seems to be using any extra equipment except for the occasional person fiddling with the Velcro on ill-fitting weighted fingerless gloves. Much like yoga, cardio kickboxing has about as much gender diversity as my eighth-grade home ec class; two men stand stolidly in the back row trying not to make eye contact with anyone else while another shuffles in at the last minute and takes the only spot left in the room, front and center.

The instructor is a woman with dark hair and olive skin who could be anywhere between twenty and sixty. She, like all community center fitness instructors it seems, polls the class for any first timers. This time, I know better than to raise my hand, but a couple in the back row with raised hands elicit the litany of instructions I imagine are reserved for the uninitiated. I listen intently, noticing the stark muscular definition of her arms as she demonstrates the four punching motions we'll use over the course of the next hour: jab, cross, hook, uppercut.

"Ready?" she asks, but doesn't wait for an answer and starts the loud warm up music, which overpowers the sound of the random female woo that pops up across the dimly-lit room. We begin by step-tapping side to side to an up-tempo remix of Lorde's "Royals." At least she's clever. We move into a series of eight right jabs, eight jumping jacks, and eight left jabs, which quickly becomes four, four, and four, then two, two, and two, then singles. I can feel my heart rate skyrocketing as my feet and arms move in tandem, my breath labored and heavy. We move into a series of right-arm-only jabs, which makes it impossible to see the instructor behind me, but to my delight I find I'm able to follow the changeups without any problem just by listening to her voice—a stark contrast from Shake & Sweat.

As we transition to the next series—right jab, left cross, right hook, left uppercut—I know that everyone else in the class is facing exactly in my direction, but somehow, I feel completely alone in my little corner, watching my form in the mirror and listening for instructions over the loud music, transitioning into David Guetta's "Titanium," one of the songs I keep on heavy rotation on my workout playlist. I already feel more like a bowl of cream of wheat than a hard metal, but I try to focus on landing my punches in the same spot, ignoring my screaming back fat.

"Jab! Cross! Hook! Upper!" the instructor repeats until she gets tired of repeating it and proceeds to launch into a pep talk.

"Keep it going," she says. "You're so strong! Look at your opponent. Your opponent is right in front of you. Make 'em pay! Do some damage!"

I note the choice to use the non-gendered pronoun given the makeup of the class participants, but dismiss the thought. I try to follow her instructions, visualizing my opponent in front of me—after all, I have a metric fuckton of visualization experience—but all I see is my own face in the mirror. My face gets harder the more I try to increase the amount of force behind my own punches, watching my right and left fists land between my mirror self's nose and chin.

"Double time to tempo, GO!" I'm rapt in the moment, so I don't even protest the two words which have recently become devil incarnate to my ears. I keep my eyes glued to my own face in the mirror, throwing punches, each harder and faster than the one before it. I'm so focused on my punches and watching my "opponent" that I don't even realize I've started crying until the tears are a steady stream down my face and my breath is coming out in whiny little whimpers. At first, I dismiss them as trickling beads of sweat and punch grunts, but then I realize my chest is heaving with more than just the increased effort to keep my heart beating. With each punch, each wave of tears that runs over my cheeks, I can feel a release of pent-up emotion that has been lying in a very long wait for an opportunity to punch its way out.

I wonder if anyone around me notices the fact that I'm in my corner blubbering like a little baby, but the music is so loud and a quick glance around the room makes me realize that everyone else is so focused on punching at imaginary adversaries or the people in front of them, no one can be bothered to notice the average-looking girl crying in the corner. I try telling myself to stop crying as we move from punches to alternating front kicks, but the tears refuse to stop coming. I surreptitiously wipe my eyes on my short sleeves with each kick, grateful both that I wore a black shirt and that it's already wet with sweat, and decide to let the release happen, let the tears just keep coming until they stop on their own. I try to remember the last time I cried, and why, but it's been so long my memory bank comes up zero balance.

The gush of tears finally stops as we put the kicking and punching combos together, but only because my heart needs to occupy the full amount of my brain power to keep up with these unfamiliar kickboxing motions, and soon there are no brain cells left to devote to crybaby behavior. The instructor stops barking punch and kick orders at us and tells us to towel off and grab a drink of water. My body is so happy to hear these instructions I feel my heart rate immediately begin to tick down as I make a beeline for the stack of stiff white community center hand towels.

I wipe my face free of tears and sweat, glad I skipped the eyeliner and mascara for my earlier trip to Dr. Kelley's office. As I bring the towel away from my face and reach for my water bottle, I notice something so odd it makes me stop mid-motion. Everyone else is the class is checking their cell phones as they towel off and hydrate. I rarely even bring mine to the gym, partially because I know they are bait to thieves like me, and partially because I don't feel the need to be constantly connected to the outside world. Is it really that hard for some people to disconnect for one measly hour?

I wait for the people stashing their phones under sweaty little gym towels uncomfortably close to my corner to finish tapping out whatever text or Facebook status update couldn't wait until after class to reclaim my spot, feeling instantly torn between wanting to deliberately smash one of these hastily-covered phones on principle, and worrying I might accidentally step on one as the instructor kicks the class up a notch and my kickboxing gets more and more clumsy.

The instructor regains everyone's attention and directs us to move into the same combo, but this time on the left side, which I know from my Shake & Sweat experience to be my bad side. Moving into position, I find that on this side of the combo I am facing everyone else instead of the wall. Although my view only includes everyone's backsides, it's still important I avoid another inner emotional episode from too much introspection, so I let my gaze wander around the room for distraction.

The guy who slipped in at the last minute a few spots down from me catches my eye. I didn't notice how good looking he was when he shuffled in before, but I do now that I see him in the zone executing the left jab, cross, hook, upper combo with precision. He has an envy-inducing golden tan and just a hint of salt-and-pepper hair at each temple. Each of his punches is form-perfect and his tank top reveals each rippling muscle group—biceps, triceps, delts, and traps—expand and contract as he moves from punch to punch.

Even in profile, I can see a fire in his dark eyes and am impressed by how into it he is. He would probably notice how blatantly I am open-mouthed staring at him if he weren't so busy staring at himself. And he's not fixated on himself in the "visualize your opponent" way the instructor suggested, but rather a "damn I look good" kind of way. For all I know, the front and center position was the only one left because the regulars in this class know it's his spot. Why are all the good-looking ones such vapid narcissists? For that matter, why are all the slightly-above-average-looking ones detectives who like model trains and could bust you for petty theft at any moment?

I shake that thought from my head and try to focus on someone else as the instructor signals for another break and everyone again dives for their cell phones. I take a big swig of my water bottle, rolling my eyes so hard it hurts, or maybe they hurt from crying. When we resume what I assume will be our last combo based on the ten minutes left on the big arm clock on the wall overhead, my eyes land on an incredibly uncoordinated woman near the back of the class. I watch her in the mirror, each motion at least a half-step behind everyone else, arms flailing like an inflatable tube man at a used car dealership. I feel both better for myself and sorry for her at the same time, wondering if this is how ridiculous I looked to everyone else in yoga, F.I.T., and Shake & Sweat.

I have to return my focus to my visible invisible opponent in the mirror as we start a series of side kicks so as not to lose my balance and topple into the older woman next to me. I wouldn't want to embarrass myself in front of Narcissus over there, though he's still so focused on smiling at himself in the mirror with his perfect, leg-muscle-accentuating side kicks he probably wouldn't notice. This time, I'm able to focus on myself without feeling any grand emotional release besides happiness. I feel so good as I imagine kicking invisible opponents on either side of me I can't help but smile at myself in the mirror and notice I'm blushing a little, whether from the gorgeous sweaty man down the row from me or from my own kickboxing prowess, I am unsure.

The instructor slows the music down just as we end a series of faster and faster kicks that sends my heart rate through the roof, and starts guiding us through stretches that feel great in a masochistic way. With each subsequent stretch, more and more people start grabbing up their cell phones and tapping away as they make an early and hasty exit. I feel my blood boil at both the disrespect of it and the fact that they're cheating themselves out of the cool down, the most important part of a workout, but maybe it's just all the blood pumping to my head from the strenuous hour of punching my own face in the mirror, kicking unseen opponents, and kneeing invisible groins.

Cell phones around my corner begin disappearing one by one, which is fine because I didn't want to steal them anyway, though I do visualize garnering some sick pleasure from the idea of depriving people so dependent on being plugged in at all times. I try to ignore the people scrambling around me to get to their phones as we move into a butterfly twist, feeling an unfamiliar rush of confidence and strength. As we stand and end the class with a final deep inhalation and exhalation exaggerated with a wide sweep of the arms, I find myself participating in the applause I always hear and usually ignore after these classes. I look in the mirror and see that I'm smiling.

The instructor chides us to stretch more at home, to hydrate, to get plenty of carbs and protein (no problem for me thanks to the takeout pasta alla nonna I'll be picking up on my way home).

"If this is your first time," she says with her eyes on the couple in the back, "I hope you'll consider making cardio kickboxing your regular Wednesday night workout."

I rotate my now-aching shoulders, feeling muscles in my back I didn't know I had. All this time I've tried to find something to target bra bulge and all I had to do was hit up cardio kickboxing. At this rate, I'll be ready for a hypothetical red carpet in no time. I smile at the instructor, and say with my mind *I just might do that.*

The filled trash bags behind the open door of Room 403 greet me as soon as I walk in my apartment with my Cheesecake Factory takeout and I realize how badly I stink. I feel enough leftover adrenaline to take out another two bags, but my protesting shoulders convince me to put this off until tomorrow. Besides, someone might see me and be suspicious that I took out so many trash bags in one day. Best not to draw suspicion, and eat copious amounts of carbs instead. Maybe even rehydrate with cheap wine.

Chapter 26

BRO DAWG DUDE BRO

Everything between my shoulder blades hurts the next day, but I still manage to haul two heavy trash bags from Room 403 out to the dumpster as soon as the sun goes down. Swinging the bags on an invisible pendulum, I build up enough inertia to hurl them on top of the weeks' worth of trash from the rest of the building, echoing with a clang as they hit the back wall of the dumpster. I remind myself that the sanitation workers who will be hauling these and the two bags from the day before won't have any interest in exploring their contents, that this is just one dumpster in an entire day's rotation. Maybe it's risky just throwing all this stolen stuff away, but no risk, no reward—that's what the motivational fitness posters at the gym say, anyway. It would only look suspicious if I came out here with a trash bag, stared at the dumpster, then chickened out and hauled the bags back up the stairs to my apartment. *You can't expect to move forward if all you're willing to do is step back.*

We're scheduled for the late game again tonight in dodgeball,

9:15 p.m., and I keep looking up at the clock in the top corner of my monitor while I mock up three boring home page designs for my boring freelance client, expecting it to be at least thirty minutes later every time so I can bill more hours and go play dodgeball with my new friends. I have both the attention span and the social agenda of a fourth grader today. I take a break from working (the third one in two hours) to lay out my outfit for dodgeball. Earlier in the day, I did a load from the overdue heap of dirty laundry specifically for my team shirt and my flame red sports bra, despite the fact that I already had a clean sports bra and no one is going to see it under my dodgeball t-shirt. I pair it with the expensive pants I bought for yoga, the ones that make me look like I have more of a Pilates butt and less of a Cheesecake Factory butt.

Technically, Joe and I still haven't really had a conversation since he had to drive me home drunk, unless you count the brief interlude after my embarrassing performance in Shake & Sweat—which I don't. I think the evening will be a success if I can just manage not to make a complete idiot of myself, not that I need another date with a police officer. In fact, if he asks me out again, I'll explain in no uncertain terms that I'm not looking for a relationship right now, that my therapist says I need to focus on myself or some such bullshit. Okay, it's not complete bullshit; I'm totally working on myself. I'll omit any details of my therapist, though. Even as I practice my one-sided response in the bathroom mirror, I find myself switching on the curling iron and applying mascara—not enough makeup to look like Penny Pintercst, but a little something to make my eyes pop, in case a rogue dodgeball knocks my glasses off my face again.

I go back to the computer only to find that a mere five minutes have passed. I try tinkering with the menu styles on one of the designs but am distracted by the tick-tick-ticking of the curling iron. I put in a couple loose curls but fail to make it look natural and start over. Why can't looking effortless actually *be* effortless? I give up and throw the whole mess up into a ponytail that looks like I tried to make a pretty ponytail. I try to go back to work but find myself just sitting and staring at the screen, mostly at the clock, which reads 7:45 p.m. I shut the lid of my laptop and decide to hit the gym early.

It's crowded for a Thursday night, and the only cardio machines available are the ones they have squeezed into random spots around the track. I opt for a stair stepper that faces the weight room although just going up and down the stairs between the first and second floor would probably be a more effective work-out. There's still over an hour until our game but at least from here I have a good view of the courts below, partially cordoned off for dodgeball. One of the teams playing now was our opponent last week. I recognize a leggy blonde with a long French braid and a strong throwing arm. From here, I'll be able to see when the first of our team arrives. Hopefully it's Officer Joe and I can have my important rehearsed conversation with him before our game, get it out of the way.

I'm five minutes into my stair stepper workout when an ear-splitting thud shakes me out of my dodgeball staring reverie and nearly knocks me off the machine. I brace myself to regain my balance, looking around to find the source of the noise. Directly in front of me in the weight room is a man with spiky hair and a ripped upper body with an otherwise flabby frame doing dead lifts in a wrestling singlet. The singlet accentuates the bulge that I did not spot intentionally but now cannot unsee. I squeeze my eyes shut, simultaneously trying to do just that and to tune out the heavy weights still bouncing loudly against the floor.

When my eyes peek open again, I see the guy using the same weights that he couldn't be bothered to lower to the ground at a reasonable volume as a chair. He removes a pair of weightlifting gloves and re-powders his hands with white dust in a tin next to the gloves. He then replaces them with another pair from a neat pile on the floor after. How many pairs of lifting gloves does one man need? He finally stands and walks in circles around the barbell, nodding politely to every man who passes by and leering creepily at every woman. Whoever designed the singlet should be executed by a firing squad.

Five full minutes pass before he does another single lift. It's enough time for me to scope out his egregious pile of equipment—extra gloves, extra shoes, a vat of protein powder, GU packets, and an array of weight lifting belts that he isn't bothering to use. As he approaches the bar, he does a series of bends at the waist—touching the bar like he's about to pick it up and then standing back up instead. Then he bounces on his tippy toes, rotating his neck as if trying to get loose, still going out of his way to acknowledge everyone who passes by. When he finally squats to pick up the bar for realsies, it's with an exaggerated series of Lamaze-type exhalations followed by a ridiculous roar as he skirts under the bar, lifting it high overhead.

If I had Jedi mind powers, I would be making the vein popping out along his left temple explode, but since I don't, I roll my eyes so hard they hurt. Even though I know it's coming, I involuntarily jump as he drops the barbell from its overhead position to the floor with another deafening, bouncing clatter. More startled people jump. I want to point to the big sign on the wall that says DO NOT DROP THE WEIGHTS. I know he would see me because he is drawing way too much attention to himself for the benefit of seeing how much everyone within earshot is noticing his "mad lifts, yo." At least, he will once he gets done high-fiving the other bro-dawgs doing dead lifts in his perimeter.

After a high five that ends in a dude-bro half hug, he turns and his eyes meet mine. I quickly return my gaze to the dodge-ball game below. None of my teammates have arrived yet. *Please don't come over here. Please don't come over here,* I repeat to myself, wanting to look up to see if he's still maintaining eye contact but not wanting to re-establish it. I look up at the useless metrics on the stair stepper. It says I've burned a whopping sixty calories, which means I can eat one of those whole wheat rolls from Cheesecake Factory, no butter. With my eyes glued to the flashing red dots, I try to focus my gaze on the dead lifter. He's still looking at me, but again fiddling with his mountain of equipment and doing laps around the barbell that I fear will fall right through the floor on his next lift, rendering our makeshift dodgeball court useless and possibly sending the blonde with the French braid to the ICU.

Before I can look back to the dodgeball court, the dead lifter locks onto me with his dude-bro tractor beam and makes his way toward me. *Crap, crap, crap.* I look back down at the controls. Sixty-three calories. Hot damn. Getting closer to that little packet of Land-o-Lakes.

"Like what you see?" he asks.

Ew. "What?" I say, pretending the Celine Dion music over-head is so loud I don't hear him.

"I said," he drawls, sauntering closer. This is even worse. "Do you like what you see?"

"Oh," I say, trying to think of what to say next when I spot a set of keys with a pink trinket of some sort between two of the lifting stations. Probably not his, unless he's also a bro-dawg with a terrible yet inflated sense of irony. "I wasn't looking at you. I was looking for my keys. There they are over there."

He's taken aback by this. How dare I not be entranced and smitten by his bro dawg guns? "Oh, I was wondering who those belonged to. I've been watching them for you."

I abandon the machine and run over to snatch the keys. I'm not stealing them; I'm just borrowing them to escape the dead lifter's tractor beam. I'll just head downstairs and turn them in to the lost and found, maybe even have some polite conversation with my new gal pal Jeanette at the front desk. I look up at the clock. 8:30 p.m. Still way too much time between now and dodgeball. Why did I come here so early when I could have gotten some more work done?

Trying to kill a fraction of it, I take my time going down the stairs and pause at every brightly-colored Comic Sans flyer on the hallway bulletin boards. My second-grade teacher would have been proud of these, but would have added one of those scalloped borders around the frame. When I reach the end of the hallway, I am relieved to see that it's Jeanette behind the desk.

"Hey, Ann!" she says with a glitter of enthusiasm. "Ready for dodgeball tonight?"

I pause, a bit surprised by her statement. Has she somehow managed to invade my daily agenda the same way I invaded hers? I must be visibly confused, because she continues.

"Your shirt. That's the—sweep the whatever—tcam, right?"

I look down at the Cobra Kai, hood spread across my boobs. Relieved, I toss the keys on the desk in front of her. "Oh, of course. Yes. We have the late game tonight. I just found these upstairs and wanted to—"

"Those must be Mrs. Waterford's keys. She's been calling about them." The deep, booming voice behind me makes the hair on the back of my neck stand up. I shouldn't have worn this stupid high cheerleader ponytail; now he can see my fear.

I turn around to face Remy, hoping my smile doesn't look too forced.

"It's awfully nice of you to return them, Miss Josephson," he continues.

Say something. Say something, I tell myself. "Have we met?" *Shit, not that, you idiot!*

He seems incensed by this, almost offended. Now he's going to think I think all black people look alike. "Of course we have, Ann. I've been seeing you come in here for weeks."

This would almost sound ominous if it weren't his job. *Think. Say something else. Something better.* "No, I mean me and Mrs. Waterford. Have we met? Sorry, I was thinking out loud there for a minute. I do that sometimes."

He smiles, a bright white smile that could be a poster in one of my dad's exam rooms, or a flyer on an elementary school nurse's bulletin board, fenced in by a primary-colored, scalloped border. "I do that sometimes, too. I'll be sure to call Mrs. Waterford and tell her the good news. She was all paranoid that someone had stolen them after the flyers someone left in the women's locker room a few weeks ago. You believe that? I told her she should be more careful about where she leaves her things laying around in here. Anyone could just walk up and take 'em."

Either he's giving me a blank look so as not to betray that he knows I am the one who's been stealing from this gym, possibly the very reason he was hired to patrol here, or he is returning the blank stare I am giving him. A wave of dread capsizes over me and I try not to let it show. He knows. He must know. That's his job. It's not like I'm *that* careful about it. I wonder if they have good Wi-Fi in prison. I realize I still haven't said anything, and he is waiting for an answer.

"I guess some people are just paranoid like that," I say, hoping it's good enough.

"I guess some people have a reason to be," he answers, smiling again. He tosses the keys between his hands as he slowly turns to walk away. My heart is in my neon vomit running shoes. Do I just stand here and wait for him to come back from the security office, which used to be a custodial closet, and haul me in to the big house? Or do I do what I always do—pretend there's nothing even remotely nefarious going on and invisibly go about the rest of my day oblivious to everyone else?

I want the keys back. I felt secure knowing that they were safely in my possession, even though I don't drive a Volkswagen or live behind the doors of the house those keys open. I realize I am frantically wringing my hands together without anything in them and probably look like a psychotic freak to my new BFF Jeanette, but I don't care. I travel to the part of my brain that stores all the mental magic Dr. Kelley has taught me about counteracting my mania—deep breathing, visualization, refuting irrational thoughts—but I struggle to put any of these into action and wonder how long I've been holding my breath.

"Hey, Ann!" A cheerful female voice from behind causes me to jump and draw the inhale I've needed for far too long. I swing around reflexively, my perky ponytail smacking me in the face and sticking to my Skittles flavored lip gloss.

"Whoa, I didn't mean to scare you." It's Sarah from dodgeball.

"No, no," I say, extracting my now-sticky curls from my lips. "You didn't scare me; I was just scaring myself." A trite line I probably heard on a movie, but in this case true nonetheless.

"Sorry we have back-to-back late games. The schedule just kinda worked out that way."

"That's okay. I don't have to be up early tomorrow." *Or ever.*

"Well, we really appreciate you filling in on the team. We're short-handed tonight so you and I will probably have to play every game."

"Short-handed?" I ask, tugging at the hem of my 50-50 blend team t-shirt. "Where's Joe?"

"Oh," she sighs, gathering her hair back in a low ponytail I imagine she won't be taking a curling iron to. "He said he's not gonna make it tonight."

Chapter 27

THE FIVE DS OF DODGEBALL

Somehow, my body acts independently from my brain through-out the games we play. My body is going through the motions of "the five Ds of dodgeball" (which, coincidentally, is the name of the opposing team): dodge, duck, dip, dive, and dodge. I'm playing well, not my initial superhero performance well, but well enough. I manage to not be the first one called out every game. I catch a couple fly balls, drop a couple fly balls, successfully dodge a couple head shots, and fail to dodge a couple line drives to the ankles.

My mind, however, is all over the goddamned place, losing its already tenuous grip on reality. It was so selfish of Joe to not be here and not tell me first so I could make up some excuse to not be here, too. I barely know these people and he had to have known I'd be uncomfortable playing here without him.

I'd asked Sarah why Joe couldn't be here, but she wasn't much help.

"Is he sick?"

"He didn't say."

"Was there a family emergency?"

"He didn't say."

"Did he get called away on a case?"

"He didn't say."

I realize this is adult recreational league dodgeball, but in my prior days of sanctioned team sports, you had to have a note from a doctor or a parent to be excused from play. You couldn't just send a text message saying "I'm not gonna make it tonight." That's just not how the world works, is it?

Surely Sarah wouldn't have been so flippant if Joe were lying paralyzed in a coma somewhere, Felicia holding his hand as he lies in a hard hospital bed, listening to the constant beep of his heart monitor. No, obviously the more likely scenario is that Joe received a phone call from Remy the community center security guard as soon as he saw me grab Mrs. Waterford's keys. Then he seized the opportunity to search my vacant apartment for the room full of bagged stolen goods, knowing I'd be otherwise occupied with his team. He knows where I live, no thanks to last week's post-dodgeball drunkenness. Maybe the whole team is in on it. Maybe he and Remy meticulously crafted the dodgeball schedule so that we'd have the late game two weeks in a row—one to take me out without the team under the guise of a school night where everyone would have an excuse to forgo after-libations, the next to break into my place under cover of nightfall. Maybe there isn't even a recreational dodgeball league and this whole thing is one big elaborate setup.

Last week's God awful second date might have just been an opportunity to make a copy of my apartment key. Maybe he'd somehow changed my order with the bartender so that I would get drunker faster. Maybe he'd paid those guys to get in a fight. No, that didn't make sense. He'd have wanted to cover his identity as a detective as long as possible. *This game really needs to end so I can rush home and catch him red-handed in my apartment trying to steal back my stolen stuff.*

The third match ends and I ask Sarah if the deal is still best three out of five. We won the first one, lost the next two.

"Hell yeah!" she says. "Still time to come back and beat these guys!"

Great. Just one more match to go and then I can hurry home. I need to get called out quickly, but not make it obvious that I am intentionally trying to get out. I make a conscious effort to bring my mind and body back together; turns out that one yoga class paid off after all. I make a feeble attempt to catch a ball flying toward me at warp speed, which sails right through my hands, into the face of the cobra emblazoned across my chest, and bounces to the floor. As I head to the sideline, I see that we have just two players left to match the opposing team's four, so the game should be over soon. As I watch each ball fly from one side of the court to the other, I try to visualize each one doing exactly what I want it to do to get this game over as quickly as possible, but my Jedi powers apparently don't work here any better than they work with bro dawgs in singlets who don't follow the rules of dead lifting.

Our two remaining players catch what should be two uncatchable balls and quickly the numbers are reversed—we have four players and they have two—and I watch my teammates divide into pairs to gang up on throwing out the last two opponents simultaneously. The rest of our team cheers as we advance to game five, while I try to keep my disappointment as buried as my feelings. I clap enthusiastically and bounce up and down, my ponytail bobbing and tugging at my scalp in a rapidly escalating hair-ache. I can't wait to rip the elastic out of my hair and shake it out, in a completely non-sexy way.

Fired up and fueled by the adrenaline of the moment, our team rallies to make quick work of our final match and vanquish our opponents. I am thrown out first by a quick shot to my blind side. I cheer from the sidelines, hoping the victory won't cause my teammates to abandon their desire for grown-up, school night responsibilities in favor of late-night celebration at JJ's. I have to get home before Joe seizes all the evidence, or if I am lucky, destroy all the evidence before Joe has a chance to discover it for himself.

I do the requisite amount of high-fiving and wait until someone else on the team—I don't remember his name—rushes out of the community center citing child bedtime duties before I move to do my own hasty exit. I start toward the front lobby in a near jog until I pass by the closed door of Remy's office, slowing my pace so as not to look suspicious. As I yank my raincoat off its hanger, a wallet from an adjacent coat falls to the floor, landing next to the hot pink sole of my shoe. I don't even glance around or open the wallet to examine its contents as I stoop to snatch it up. I just drop it in my jacket pocket as naturally as though it were mine, which it now is. As if a light switch had just been flipped, I feel all the anxiety that's been building inside me over the possibilities of Joe's whereabouts go dark and quiet.

The brief feeling of peace lasts about as long as it takes me to drive home. By the time I sprint from my car through the pouring rain and climb the stairs to my apartment, I am greeted not by Average Joe rifling through my apartment, but by the horror that is my once-manicured ponytail, now dripping with rainwater in stringy clumps. That, paired with the realization that I just took what is essentially someone's life in a four-inch-by-four-inch square burning a hole in my jacket pocket. I don't need it any more than I needed a set of keys that don't open anything I own. I hadn't even thought for a second about keeping the keys, not until Remy walked up and taunted me. My painful ponytail is even more painful to dislodge with the elastic wound so tightly around wet hair.

I open the wallet but for some reason I already know whose unsmiling face will greet me before I see it under the big banner of the Kansas driver's license. Remy Blaylock: organ donor, Johnson County resident, six-foot-two, thirty-seven-year-old male. Security guard at the Percival O'Shaughnessy Community Center circa February of this year. Southwest Airlines and Sears card holder.

I slam the wallet and my own eyes closed, realizing that my new conspiracy theory held a lot more water than the one I'd entertained just moments ago. He baited me. He had to have known that I would take it. He had to have recognized the fake Burberry raincoat I'd already taken from someone else and planted his wallet there to see if I would take the bait. It was a risky move on his part, and I had to give him props for that, but I imagine outside of pursuing the elusive community klepto, his job affords little in the way of excitement.

I can't deal with the wallet right now, and I can't put my original plan into action (destroy all the evidence before Officer Joe can find it) because it's pouring rain. The only thing more suspicious than taking an entire room full of trash bags out to the dumpster is taking an entire room full of trash bags out to the dumpster in a torrential downpour. I enter Room 403 to verify it hasn't been disturbed since I last came in here to grab two bags to bring them down to the dumpster. The sudden vibration of my phone in my back pocket is deafening against the silence of the apartment and violent against my ass, which is in an amount of trouble I don't really want to consider. I instinctively jump in alarm.

It's a text message from Joe, and it just says, "Hey u. Sorry I couldn't make it 2nite. Did we win?"

Is he fucking with me? Maybe he really has no idea that I'm the community center's most wanted. Maybe he and Remy aren't in cahoots after all. Then again, maybe he's just playing his cards close to the chest. Isn't that his job? It still doesn't explain why he skipped out on dodgeball tonight without telling me. I should answer.

"We sure did! High fives all around. Everything ok?"

I stand in the doorway of Room 403 staring at my phone, waiting for him to respond. The longer I stand here, the longer I don't have to take these bags out to the trash or look at the wallet or figure out what I'm going to do with it.

"Yah. Thought somethin big was goin down at the station, but false alarm."

Is he baiting me like Remy did? Does he expect me to walk through the rain and up the steps of the police station to turn myself in, like something out of a bad '80s crime drama? Wouldn't be the first time I've been baited today, and at least now I can respond.

"You coulda told me you weren't gonna be there."

I consider telling him that I got all gussied up for him and he missed out, but this would just come across as bitchy flirting–the worst possible kind. As I stand and wait for him to respond, I wonder how long Remy plotted to put his plan into action. He had to have known that at 9:45 p.m. on a Thursday, there wouldn't be enough people around that the wallet would risk being stolen by anyone other than the dodgeball crew, and he had to be relying on the basic decency of human beings to turn in a lost wallet. Unless he really just lost it because he's secretly an absent-minded security guard.

"Sorry, but that's the job. What do u expect from me?"

I respond immediately.

"I expect common courtesy."

He responds immediately back.

"So do I. Maybe that's 2 much 2 ask. Call me when your ready for that."

Maybe he doesn't know after all. Maybe he still wants to give me the benefit of the doubt. After all, he can't even use the right form of *your/you're*; why should he figure out that I have a room full of things that I've stolen from people at the gym over the past three years? I look out at the rain and feel every ounce of the melancholy that comes with it. I finally manage to find someone willing to put up with me, and I fuck it up. I finally start to make real progress toward managing my disorder and with one snap decision, erase all progress and put myself back in real jeopardy. I need help. I need to call Dr. Kelley. But first, I need to figure out what I'm going to do with this goddamned wallet, and keep the two-a-day promise to myself and haul these bags out to the dumpster in the pouring rain. You never see that in movies.

Chapter 28

MAC ATTACK

I don't end up calling Dr. Kelley or anyone else. I keep staring at my phone, waiting for an olive branch in the form of a text message from Joe, but it doesn't come, and I'm not about to cry uncle first. Instead, I sit alone in my apartment for three straight days, talking only to the pizza man who has come by twice in that time to deliver me breakfast, lunch, and dinner. The rain has not stopped, not even long enough for me to take any trash bags out to the dumpster. I tip the pizza guy extra because of the constant rain dripping from the brim of his Papa John's ball cap and consider asking if he'd accept a little extra to take my trash bags out for me, but decide against it. This is still my battle to fight, and I'll keep fighting it if it ever stops raining.

Remy's wallet is sitting in the same kitchen drawer as the wax paper and aluminum foil I never use. The idea was "out of sight, out of mind," but this sounded far easier than it's been in practice. It's the first thing I think about the moment free brain space opens up, which is pretty often since I'm alone and self-barricaded in my apartment. I can't talk to anyone, can't go to the community center, and can't think, so I work. I bill an impressive twenty-eight hours between Friday, Saturday, and Sunday and by the time Monday morning rolls around, I've sent a final invoice for the client I've been putting off for weeks, submitted proposals on eLance for four other clients, and managed to clear out all but five emails out of my inbox, which I will follow up on before the end of the day.

Despite the slate gray skies and the lake in my parking lot, my mood is bolstered by the level of professional productivity I feel. Now that I've finished that, I can push the play button on the plan to get rid of the Room 403 bags and figure out what to do with the wallet. Who says I need my therapist for this? I've got it under complete control. I haul two bags out to the dumpster even though it's still raining steadily, and immediately need a shower after I do so. Feeling clean, accomplished, and of a semi-sound mental state (all things considered), I sit down in front of my computer to address the five email follow-ups which are long overdue, squeezing the excess water out of my hair with a red towel, only to find that three new emails have threatened my impressive progress toward inbox level zero.

One is from my alma mater: "Please donate money you could be using to pay off the student loans you took out to attend our fine institution." One is from Adobe Creative Cloud: "You've been using our product (and running our hourly updates) a lot in the past few days. Perhaps you'd like to upgrade for the low low price of $99.99!" The final one is from my newly-former client: "Re: Invoice 12123."

Thank you for submitting invoice #12123 for this project; however, we cannot pay this invoice at this time due to the fact that we terminated our contract with you on 3/3 due to a lack of demonstrable progress as per the contract on the agreed project plan. Below you'll find the correspondence we sent on this date communicating termination of this contract. Thanks again, and we wish you well in your future endeavors.

A bubble bursts inside my chest. I search my Trash folder for the email they say they sent and sure enough, there it is. I've been fired for almost forty-five days and I didn't even know it. Guess I shouldn't have Ctrl+A'd that list of emails I didn't think was important. I stomp off to the kitchen and yank the wallet drawer open, extracting Remy's community center member card out of its slot. Surely, he would be monitoring the security system for use of my own, but he has to use his all the time. The only thing that can clear my head now is kickboxing.

I manage to enter the community center and duck into kickboxing class without incident. If Remy is here, he's locked in his windowless office and I can only hope that he has better things to do than watch the access logs. Otherwise, I cling to the hope that he's at Sears convincing the clerks that he really does have a Sears card, his wallet was just stolen by a skinny, average-looking white girl. Kickboxing does make me feel better, though I find myself once again fighting back tears and staring myself down, red-faced in the mirror.

I saunter out behind the narcissistic guy whose repeat performance I enjoyed in class. I look for an inconspicuous spot in the warmup area where I can do a few post-workout stretches. The extent of my physical activity for the past three days has caught up to me and I feel like I could nap for days. I stroll up to the stack of rubber mats, hoping I won't contract Ebola from whatever is on the sticky floor and that the pair of high school age girls sitting on top of the pile of mats tapping away on their phones will get the hint and move so I can grab one. I stand awkwardly in front of them for several seconds, but they're so focused on their phones they don't even notice me. I start to feel my blood boiling and take a deep, cleansing breath, which has the added benefit of being audible enough for the girls to notice and look at me, annoyed that I am interrupting.

"Excuse me," I say in the friendliest voice I can muster behind my fake smile.

The girls look at one another and giggle. What is it about high school girls that makes everything so giggle-worthy?

"What?" the blonde on the left says.

"Can I grab one of those mats, please?" I ask, growing more exasperated by the second but praising myself for positively managing my anxiety and taking the high road. They stand up with a melodramatic degree of effort, as though I'd just asked them to help me retrieve an eighty-pound boulder from the top shelf at Target. I give them a tight-lipped smile and a curt "thank you." I start to walk away but turn around, feeling like it's my duty as someone older and wiser to both assert myself and dispense valuable life advice.

"You know, studies show that the average gymgoer wastes as much as thirty-five percent of their workout by playing on the phone." This is met by an open-mouthed gawk from one, an annoyed glare from the other.

"Just sayin'," I say, turning around and walking away.

The warmup area has filled up with other post-kickboxing members looking to cool down, so the only somewhat hidden spot is the area next to Mac. I call him Mac because he always brings in his entire expensive Macbook Pro setup—laptop, stand, monitor, speakers—and watches a video of some meathead counting out his reps for him and giving him "attaboys." If you're going to bring all the comforts of home to the gym, then why not just work out at home? The only way it could be more ridiculous would be if Arnold Schwarzenegger were the host and the background music was "Don't Stop Believin'," both of which in this case are true.

I'm not sure how he can maintain his focus on his workout, his virtual instructor, the Journey chorus, and whoever it is he's talking to loudly over the phone on his Bluetooth headset, but somehow, he does. Given the volume at which he is talking, there must be a direct correlation between physical concentration and microphone shouting. I shake the mat out as loudly as possible as I claim the spot next to him, hoping he'll be clued in to the fact that there are other people around him who can hear in great detail the subject of his conversation, which has something to do with selling a condo and getting a colonoscopy, hopefully not in the span of the same day.

I close my eyes and lie back on the mat, hugging my knees into my chest, rocking back and forth to massage the spine I just made do a lot of work. Just like I learned in yoga class, I try to tune out the obnoxiously loud phone conversation and Austrian accent counting coming from the speakers. Visualizing—the therapist's version of going to my happy place—so as to not let my urges get the best of me. I flip over onto my belly so I can survey the rest of the gym, so far, no sign of Remy or any other community center staffer. Lucky for me, Monday is a busy night here, and I can blend in easily enough. Added bonus—Average Joe never comes to the gym on Mondays.

I decide to take a risk and head to the weight machine area to bang out a few reps while everyone is too busy stepping over each other to notice me, but I keep my mat laid out so I can come back to it, hopefully undisturbed, in a few minutes. I hover around the bench presses, waiting to see who will finish first so I can swoop in as soon as he's done. A youngish guy at the far end begins to sit up and I casually walk over, grabbing two fifteen-pound weights off the rack and waiting for him to remove his, which are substantially heavier.

Instead, he shakes his arms out as he sits all the way up, then proceeds to grab his phone from the floor beside him. He flexes one arm then extends his phone out with the other, smiling wide as he snaps a picture. I roll my eyes and set my thirty pounds down as gently as I can, but audibly enough that he'll get the hint that taking selfies while someone is waiting for you to finish is bad gym etiquette. Everyone knows that.

"Are you finished?" I ask politely but firmly.

"Almost," he says without looking at me, prepping for another camera shot. The first one must not have been good enough.

"Are you doing another set right now?" I ask, more sternly than before.

"Nah, just Instagramming. Gimme a minute."

I can only imagine that instead of helping an obviously waiting woman with thirty pounds of weight plates, he'd rather hashtag #nbd or #crushedit or #swole to impress the ladies who are also too busy live tweeting their workouts to actually work out. I'm a young whippersnapper, here. I'm supposed to be the one old folks complain about, not the one shaking my fist and yelling "Get off my lawn!" Metaphorically of course.

"Okay, I'm done," he says, darting off to another machine without making eye contact.

"Hey," I yell after him, "aren't you gonna rack your weights?"

He returns what I can only assume is an obviously annoyed glare with a blank look. "The person *after* you is supposed to do that."

"No, they're not," I call after him, but he's already tuned me out and is trotting off to annoy someone else. I haul his forty-five-pound plates to the rack with an exasperated sigh as musclebound men pass by me left and right but are too busy staring at their phones to notice that I could use a little help. If Joe were here, I realize with a sinking heart, he'd cut across the track to help me. I was awful and vindictive to him, and it was over text message of all things. It dawns on me how much I've missed him over the last couple days—not because of the constant rain or because I've been alone, but because he reminds me that people can be decent, because I'm not an anxiety-addled hot mess when I'm around him. Not all the time, anyway. I sigh audibly, realizing I need to be the bigger person and apologize. But I'll wait until after I get home, because some of us have the ability to leave the phones in our locker while we go work out. #JustSayin.

I try to get two sets in, but my arms aren't very forgiving to me after taking three days off then wearing my new pair of weighted gloves (that are pink and sort of resemble a vulva) in kickboxing. After a set of ten and five more reps after that, I give up and head back to the warmup area (but not before racking my weights like a decent human being). My mat is undisturbed, but Mac is still talking on the phone oblivious to everyone around him, though the crowd has thinned somewhat.

"Hey, hold on a sec," I hear him say as he bends over to pause the video and unzip his backpack, ass in my direction. "I've gotta take a piss."

I roll over to my side, both to block him out and to stretch one leg across my body, but Mac is having none of it.

"Watch my stuff, will ya, doll?" he asks, stepping over me without making eye contact. I squeeze my eyes shut so I can't see up his loose basketball shorts. I feel my pulse quickening and actively breathe in and out with exaggerated inhalations and exhalations to calm myself, but it doesn't work. I draw the opposite leg across my body and my gaze falls on the empty backpack and unattended audio-video setup. I take a quick glance around, even though this is tantamount to breaking the first rule of Fight

Club, but as expected, everyone is either too busy with their workouts or staring at their tiny screens to notice me.

I act quickly, stuffing the Macbook Pro and peripherals into the backpack without even disconnecting them from each other. Everything barely fits inside and weighs nearly as much as the weights I was holding while waiting for the bench press. I feel the new pain in my shoulders as I heave the straps onto my back and jog toward the stairs, not bothering to wipe down my mat and return it to the pile. What's the point? No one else is following the rules posted on the cinderblock wall.

I extract the rest of my stuff from my locker as quickly as possible, tapping out a text message to Joe as I make my hasty exit.

"We should talk."

Chapter 29

EARL GREY

For the fourth day in a row, the rain is still steadily coming down when I pull in to my apartment parking lot next to a car I fail to recognize until its driver is already opening my door. A heart attack subsides as I realize it's Joe, the consummate chivalrous gentleman, shielding my exit with a large black umbrella.

"What are you doing here?" I ask, practically shouting over the rain, pelting the pavement with loud taps.

"You said you needed to talk," he answers, flashing the smile that will definitely be the end of me. "I have the day off since it's Memorial Day."

"I said we *should*–talk. And I meant on the phone or something. Not at my apartment. Not in person."

"Well, I wanted to see you," he says, inching toward the rear driver's side door and bringing me with him. "Let me help you with this stuff."

Even with the umbrella, the rain is so relentless that we're both still getting soaked. He opens the door and reaches for both my duffel bag and the backpack with Mac's Mac. I jolt into action.

"I've got it; that's okay." I snatch up the backpack and slip it over my rain-drenched shoulders, trying not to betray how heavy it is. I let him grab the duffel bag only because I know protesting will be more effort than it's worth.

"Let's get inside," he says, moving in closer with the umbrella. *Don't panic*, I tell myself over and over until we reach the covered stairwell.

"I'd invite you in, but it's really messy," I say. I start to take mental inventory of the state of the apartment. The stolen wallet is back in the kitchen drawer, behind the wax paper and aluminum foil. The door to Room 403 is closed. I try to think of anything out in the open that would greet Joe's suspicion, but come up empty. Still, the last thing I want right now is to let him inside.

"You'd rather talk out here? It's pouring rain! I'm not gonna let you stand out here and catch cold." He collapses the umbrella, shakes the water loose, and props it up next to the door, waiting for an invitation.

Think. Think. I have to play it cool. If I protest too much, he'll know something's up, but how can I possibly fool a detective?

"Okay," I finally relent, twisting the key in the lock and praying that I didn't leave a bra on the floor or something in my post-email delirium. I inch the door open, checking to verify the coast is clear, before I swing it wide and nod for him to go in.

"No, you first."

Of course. I walk in and start to shrug off the backpack.

"Let me help you with that," he says, reaching for the straps with a gentle touch that lightly brushes my shoulders. I let him, hopeful my cooperation will dismiss any suspicion that might arise from the weight of the bag.

"Jesus, what do you have in this thing? Bricks?" he asks with a grunt and a laugh, setting the bag down with a soft thud that makes me nervous even though I never intend to use the computer.

"Dumbbells," I answer, but not too quickly.

"The taxpayer-provided dumbbells not good enough for ya?"

"Nope," I say, crossing to the bathroom and grabbing two towels. I hand one to him.

"Thanks," he says, running the towel over his head for long enough that it gives me a second to look around while his eyes are shielded. I smile as he hands it back.

"I feel like this rain's never gonna end," I say, taking a page out of my mother's conversation handbook. Weather is her favorite topic. Next, I should shove a glass of wine in his face.

"Yeah," he says with a curt nod that makes it clear he's not interested in talking about the weather.

"I don't really have anything to drink, except maybe some tea," I say.

"Tea sounds nice."

I make my way to the kitchen, fighting the urge to pause in front of the drawer holding Remy's wallet and stand there until I can convince him to leave. I fill the kettle and watch Joe out of the corner of my eye. He's surveying the apartment, but less like a cop and more like a friend over for the first time. I try to think of the last time someone besides me was in this apartment. It was probably the maintenance guy last summer when someone hit a baseball through my bedroom window.

"Chamomile or Earl Grey?"

"Doesn't matter."

I drop a bag of Earl Grey into his cup and chamomile into mine—both mugs courtesy of Josephson Smiles Family Dentistry. I don't need the caffeine to add any more jitteriness to what I'm already feeling on the inside and hope I'm successfully hiding on the outside. I want him to be looking around my apartment making me uncomfortable, but I have no pictures on my wall and all my furniture is IKEA. So instead, he's staring at me and making me uncomfortable.

"It'll just take a minute for the water to boil," I say.

"All right," he says before a pregnant pause. "You said you wanted to talk?"

I nod. "I owe you an apology." The words come out soft and nervous, which isn't an act.

"An apology for what?" he says. He's going to make me say it. It's a tactic my father always used when I got in trouble as a kid.

"I was rude to you when you texted the other day. I was upset that you didn't tell me you wouldn't be at the game."

He nods. "You were uncomfortable without me there?"

"Yes."

"Well I accept your apology, and I apologize that I made you uncomfortable."

"Okay." A long silence follows. I don't know if that means we're cool or if there's more; I don't exactly have a boatload of experience in this arena. I decide to let him break the silence.

"Anything else?" he asks, crossing his arms over his chest.

"No," I say, smiling feebly.

"You don't want to apologize for anything else?"

I meet his confused look with one of my own. "Apologize for what?"

"Oh, I don't know, Ann," he says, uncrossing his arms and taking two steps closer to me. I can just detect a hint of his signature eau-de-Led-Zeppelin. For a second, I think he's moving in to kiss me, but then I see him reach inside his windbreaker. "You could apologize for stealing my phone."

This is it. I've had nightmares about being confronted by someone I stole from, but in my scariest dreams there was never a cop standing less than arm's length in front of me in my own living room. I don't know what to say, so I don't say anything. He removes a tri-folded sheet of paper from his windbreaker.

"I have a warrant to search the premises." He tries to hand it to me but somewhere between my brain and my arms the message to take it is lost. He sets it on the kitchen counter behind me. The teakettle begins to whistle behind me, but I still can't move. Joe moves two steps closer and puts his hands on my shoulders.

"It's going to be okay, Ann. Let me get the tea."

I know it's his job, but I can't help but be impressed by his poised demeanor under pressure, especially since I am freaked out to the point of catatonia. He calmly pours the tea into the respective mugs and sets mine in front of me, the two of us separated by the kitchen counter.

"You knew?" I ask, staring down at the growing hazel clouds in my steeping tea, unable to make eye contact.

"I knew," he says.

"The whole time?"

"No, not the whole time. I didn't know about the phone until a few days ago."

"So, they really have detectives on the job to case petty thieves at the community center?" It sounds so ridiculous as I say it that it comes out with a half-hearted laugh.

"Well," he says, taking a sip of the too-hot tea, "until the opioid epidemic hits Johnson County . . ."

I manage to laugh a little, which was probably his tactic. Get me to relax.

"Not really. I just happen to have lunch once a month with the director over at Parks and Rec. They'd had complaints of people getting little things stolen here and there, but once bigger things started to go missing—iPads, smartphones—" he pauses, forcing me to make eye contact, "—pearl necklaces."

I swallow a mouthful of shame.

"They started thinking a crime syndicate was moving in. I told them they were being ridiculous but I said I'd look into it anyway as a favor. And I told them to hire a security guard."

"Remy."

"Remy. Whose wallet disappeared under suspicious circumstances the night of our dodgeball game. He'd suspected you from day one but I told him he was crazy."

"So, you got close to me," I say, watching the shame wave turn to him.

"So I got close to you. I'm sorry. I didn't think this . . . whatever it is . . . would happen; I really didn't."

"Did you ever like me?" I say, in a voice that comes out far more schoolgirl-dumped-at-the-prom than I mean for it to.

"I did, Ann. I really did."

"But when you kept asking me to go out with you, it wasn't because you wanted to really get to know me better. It was because you wanted to know what I knew."

He pauses, tight-lipped. "Yes, that's partly true. I wasn't looking for a relationship."

"Because you already have one," I say, blinking back the tears in my eyes. "Felicia, right?"

"Felicia and I—it's complicated," he says.

"That your Facebook relationship status?" I snap back.

"You have my phone," he says, recrossing his arms. "You should know."

I suppose I deserved that. "Had. I *had* your phone. So, what happens now?" I take a big swallow of my tea, hoping it will burn the tears away.

"Well, this warrant was requested Friday after the wallet

went missing, but the judge didn't get it to me until today. Either I can search this place or you can cooperate and show me where everything is."

I look up at him, but only barely. "Everything?"

"Everything. And let me be clear, I highly recommend you take the cooperative route. It'll make things a lot easier on you."

I feel a tear fall from my eye. I see him start to reach out to wipe it away, but he stops and retreats, probably remembering that I'm his suspect in the middle of a half-hearted confession.

"I can explain," I say, catching a whiff of the sweaty clothes that I realize I am still wearing.

"Don't," he says, voice edgy and defensive. "I don't want you to explain, and you really shouldn't say anything else to me. Not without an attorney present. Just show me the stuff and we'll go from there."

I wipe my eyes and heave the backpack onto the kitchen counter, backing away with an implicit invitation. I let him unzip it. He sighs heavily.

"I received a call right after your text message about this. It's why I came over."

"I'm sorry."

He straightens, suddenly all business. "Where's the rest?"

I motion for him to follow me to Room 403, where I point to the door and turn so I don't have to see it, resting my head against the adjacent wall. I try to read his expression out of the corner of my eye, but I can't.

"That everything?" he asks without looking at me.

"There are a couple bags in the dumpster outside."

"My phone?" he asks flatly.

"I destroyed it. A couple weeks ago."

He clears his throat. "Okay. Anything else?"

I shrug myself off the wall and cross back into the kitchen.

He starts to follow me but pauses on my desk chair, where his cardigan lies in a rumpled heap. He glares at me as he rolls it up like the team t-shirt he gave me a couple weeks ago, stuffs it under one arm, and joins me in the kitchen. I grip the handle to the drawer but I can't bring myself to open it.

"Let me," he says. When I tighten my grip, he gently grabs my wrist and eases the drawer open. I wish I didn't want him to touch me so badly. I wish he didn't have to see me like this, both of us looking down at the wallet, knowing exactly what it represents. He lets go of me even though I'm willing him not to. Our eyes meet, a reciprocal knowing look that doesn't need to verbalize what's next.

"Can I at least change out of my sweaty clothes first?" I ask.

He smiles, unwillingly I can tell. "Sure. But don't try anything funny. I know you don't have any registered firearms; I'm not going to find any un-registered ones, am I?"

I shake my head, and at his nod, hurry off to my bedroom. As soon as I close the door, I hear Joe on his phone. I can't make out much beyond "suspect in custody." I throw on a clean-ish pair of jeans over my shoes, wriggle into a hoodie, and twist my sweaty, rainy hair up into a top knot before grabbing a purse and making sure I have everything in it. Surely Mom and Dad have some lawyers in their circles of friends, assuming they'll want anything to do with me once they get a call from the police station. After all, it would require them making a trip to North Johnson County. The horror.

"Do me one favor?" I say to Joe, who is waiting by the door with an open pair of handcuffs. In another life, this scene might be kinky instead of ominous.

"What?"

"Call my parents. I don't want them to hear it from someone else."

He nods in agreement and holds up the handcuffs. "I don't need to use these, do I?"

I shake my head no, and let him lead me out the apartment, gently holding my aching bicep and locking the doorknob behind me. He re-opens the umbrella, huddling next to me as we descend the stairs.

"Felicia's a lucky lady, you know," I say, wishing we were walking through the rain sharing an umbrella under different circumstances.

He laughs a little, smiling down at me. "She doesn't seem to think so."

EPILOGUE

REDEMPTION THONG

"Hello?" I say breathlessly into the phone, running from the bathroom still dripping with water.

"Hey, Klepto," says the voice on the other end. He's taken to calling me that.

I smile, but he can't hear that. "Hey."

"I'll be by to pick you up in an hour. That enough time for you?"

"Yeah, sure."

"Okay, great. I gotta go. See you in a few."

"Okay. Bye."

I finish toweling off, using one of two towels I've managed to unpack since moving to Overland Park. It's Law Enforcement Appreciation Day at the K, and Joe offered up a free ticket and a drive out to Kauffman Stadium for today's early afternoon game. It took me most of yesterday ripping apart boxes to find the one Royals shirt I own, and have since high school.

It's been ten months since my arrest last Memorial Day. My

parents didn't end up disowning me after all, which is a good thing because I got kicked out of my apartment for violating the lease's illegal activity clause (though I think that was primarily put in there for meth heads) and had to live in my old room at their house for a while—in the part they refer to as "the East wing" as if they reside in Wayne Manor or something. They fronted my $1000 bail and got me a good Brooks Brothers–wearing defense attorney, one of the husbands from my mom's Junior League chapter. Besides having to live with them for the better part of a year, paying them back everything they spent on my legal fees, and getting a real job, the only other punishment from my parents was joining my mom's Advocare team as an independent distributor. I'm really, really terrible at shilling snake oil supplements, and I mostly just buy them for myself, but it keeps her off my back.

Johnson County was less lenient with me, though it certainly could have been worse. Dr. Kelley's testimony as my therapist proved to be instrumental in convincing the judge that I had (and have) a condition, that I didn't just steal from all those people because I'm a marginally pretty little white girl who thought I could get away with it. Even Joe went to bat for me, testifying about how I willingly surrendered and cooperated fully in his investigation, which probably took him all of twelve minutes.

On my twenty-sixth birthday, I received a sentence of three years supervised probation, 1,000 hours of community service (which is just as many hours as it sounds like), plus I have to pay for all the things I stole that weren't returned to their rightful owners. That should only take me until my thirtieth birthday, give or take, depending on the rate of inflation. Joe's best friend is a probation officer, and Joe pulled some strings to get me on his service. He's a nice enough guy, doesn't give me too hard a time, even when Joe tries to provoke him by telling the story about how I stole his cardigan and his cell phone. It's a story that gets more blown out of proportion every time he tells it; currently, we're up to me using the cardigan as a pillowcase and racking up charges from calling psychic hotlines.

I was also banned permanently from the Percival O'Shaughnessy Community Center. I would have been more incensed about this part of the sentence if they hadn't cut the city's budget for rec league dodgeball, putting Sweep the Ball, Johnny on an indefinite hiatus. Mom and Dad pressed for me to join their country club, but I refused. The community center in Overland Park is just like Percival O'Shaughnessy, but the pool's bigger and they have surveillance cameras. I couldn't steal anything and get away with it even if I wanted to, which I don't. For my community service, I lifeguard and teach swim lessons at the center. Everyone assumes I'm just another one of the high school students lifeguarding for extra cash, not a convicted criminal serving out my sentence one boring three-hour block at a time. I let them keep their illusions and enjoy yelling at children to stop running. People look at me like I'm a sociopath if I do that outside of lifeguarding.

I still go see Dr. Kelley once a week as per the terms of my probation. She's been far more clinical and distant with me ever since I got arrested and drug her into my legal proceedings. I think it's because the judge publicly chastised her for not coming forward with my wrongdoing, doctor–patient confidentiality notwithstanding. She still cashes my check every week, though, so she wasn't butthurt enough about it to drop me as a client. My parents make me pay for it now.

Dr. Kelley's check is just one of the ones I write out begrudgingly week after week as a constant reminder of my own stupidity. My big-girl job doing design for the marketing division at National Pizza Company keeps me afloat with my many creditors. The logo for Pizza Hut's reboot of the Big New Yorker? That was me. I also had a hand in the architecture and logo redesign for all the Wendy's franchises, but I can't take complete credit for that one.

The only pair of clean underwear I can find is the white thong my mom bought me my senior of high school so I wouldn't have visible panty lines in my prom picture. Tomorrow, I really need to find some time to seriously tackle unpacking more boxes. Between a full-time job, counseling sessions, community service, probation officer meetings, and my own gym schedule, I haven't had time for much of anything else. I'm pretty sure that was the judge's idea, idle hands being the devil's playground and all. I squirm into the thong and finish blow-drying my hair, counting down the minutes until Joe's arrival.

Joe is chauffeuring three other people to the K, so I end up sitting behind him in the back seat, keeping to myself but chatting politely with the others, who I've met before in passing. I get to sit next to him in the stadium seats that are really close together, which makes me happy. I get to watch him having fun, which means I'll get to watch him smile a lot. That smile still slays me, and I think it always will.

It took a while for Joe to come to terms with what I did to him and forgive me; we had lots of time to talk during my stints at the police station last summer. He and Felicia are in an off-again stage in the saga that is their on-again, off-again relationship. Joe doesn't really talk about it, but I'm working on honing my Jedi mind powers to hopefully make the two of us an item somewhere down the road. For now, I'm just happy to have a friend who gets me and keeps me accountable, which is what I think Dr. Kelley was going for when she prescribed dodgeball and other group classes last year. She certainly wasn't going for a class C misdemeanor.

I inconspicuously wash down my Ativan with a twelve-dollar stadium beer after downing two hot dogs in the seventh inning, when they announced that they were selling them for a buck apiece until they were gone. On my way back to my seat, I shuffled past a woman who looked a lot like Jeanette, but wasn't upon closer inspection (luckily for me, as this would have violated the "never come near me again" policy she'd laid out shortly after my release from custody). The meds do help me manage the anxiety that Dr. Kelley says triggered my kleptomania, but I swear they also make me see people I know left and right. That's a side effect they don't list on the very scary box.

"Hey, Klepto," Joe says, shaking me out of my thoughts and my vacant stare at the way the first baseman looks in his polyester pants. If I got paid a bjillion dollars to basically work out, I'd have a really fabulous ass, too.

"Hmm?" I say, still trying to swallow the big fat pill.

"You've got mustard on your face." He reaches up with a napkin and a "May I?" gesture which I acquiesce with a nod. He gently swabs my cheek with the napkin I wish wasn't separating my face from his hand and smiles.

"All better," he says, putting an arm around me that's more I'm-about-to-give-you-a-noogie than it is romantic, but I'll take it. I smile back at him and say thanks, squirming as my thong reminds me that it's still there and riding uncomfortably up. If I can't have Joe, I guess I'll just return to my infielder fantasies for the time being. The family in the seats to the opposite side of me begins to gather their things to leave. It's the bottom of the eighth inning on a school night, the Royals are up four runs, and they have four young kids with them that I imagine they would rather not sit in traffic with for hours; they must be from Johnson County.

"Enjoy the rest of the game," the person I assume to be the dad says to me as they climb over us and into the aisle. I look over and see a well-worn baseball glove that was hoping to catch a high foul ball that never came. There's still time for me to shout out "Wait! You've left your glove!" But I don't. Instead, I find myself looking longingly at the rough leather despite having absolutely zero practical use for a baseball glove of my own. I start to tell myself a story about how it's the glove my dad gave me when I told him I wanted to try out for softball back in junior high (which I did, and still remember with vivid embarrassment as I took an easy pop fly right on the bridge of my nose). *Yes, I brought it with me to the stadium, I just forgot I had it until now, that's all,* I rehearse saying in case Joe asks me about it.

It's not really stealing if someone leaves it behind, is it?

THE END

ACKNOWLEDGMENTS

I t takes a village to raise a book, and I've been raising this one longer than I've been raising my children. They get the first thank you, for eventually figuring how to sleep so Mom could get some writing done, and constantly giving me hilarious ideas for future novels.

This book would have never been possible without the people who came to the Weird Austin Writers workshop group at the Monkey Nest week after week and month after month, like the masochists they were, critiquing chapter after chapter and encouraging me to keep going. Weird Austin Writer regulars like Tobias Garrett, Eric Edge, and Leticia Estavillo made my manuscript the strongest it could be and helped me avoid plot holes bigger than Ann's pile of stolen junk.

I'll be forever grateful to the crew at She Writes Press for taking a chance on me and giving me my first "big" book deal: from Brooke Warner, my project manager Samantha Strom, and editor Elisabeth Kauffman, to all the folks behind the scenes, and especially the design team who made the cover for *Community Klepto* the gorgeous runway model it is. I felt like a total impostor when I submitted my book to the 2019 Independent Publisher of the Year, but it's been a fantastic experience from start to finish.

Thank you to my publicity team, Rick and Caitlin Hamilton Summie, for knowing how to make my book successful in the marketplace and helping me plan a badass in-person book launch after two years of COVID despair isolation. Thank you to Zibby Owens for giving me a voice on *Moms Don't Have Time to Write* and elevating the profile of books and authors everywhere.

Thanks to all the people who inspired and entertained me at the gyms I've frequented over the years, even the assholes who felt the need to stop me while I was marathon training to tell me I shouldn't have been out running by myself. Glad I didn't get murdered so I could call you all out in humorous fashion. A first position pulsing thank you to Lauren Whitehead, the barre instructor who always gives me fodder for my next writing project while kicking my ass, and a happy baby thank you to Jeff Cattan, the yoga instructor who's made me laugh, cry, and fart—often in the same class.

Finally, thank you to my husband Mike for always being in my corner, for putting the twins back to bed for the ninety-eighth time so I could get my dedicated writing time in, and for laughing at most of my jokes, even when they're terrible (actually, especially when they're terrible). I love you and your dad jokes. Thanks, beeb.

ABOUT THE AUTHOR

Kelly I. Hitchcock is a literary fiction author and poet who lives in the Austin, Texas, area. She has published several poems, short stories, and creative non-fiction works in literary journals and is the author of the coming-of-age novel *The Redheaded Stepchild*, a semi-finalist in the literary category for The Kindle Book Review's "Best Indie Books of 2011," and *Portrait of Woman in Ink: A Tattoo Storybook*. Her work has appeared in *Clackamas Literary Review* and *Foliate Oak Literary Journal*, in anthologies by Line Zero and Alien Buddha Press, and more. Kelly holds a BA in creative writing from Missouri State University. She has five-year-old identical twins and a full-time job, so writing and picking up LEGO are the only other things she can devote herself to.

SELECTED TITLES FROM SHE WRITES PRESS

She Writes Press is an independent publishing company
founded to serve women writers everywhere.
Visit us at www.shewritespress.com.

Royal Entertainment by Marni Fechter. $16.95, 978-1-938314-52-0. After
being fired from her job for blowing the whistle on her boss, social
worker Melody Frank has to adapt to her new life as the assistant to an
elite New York party planner.

Size Matters by Cathryn Novak. $16.95, 978-1-63152-103-4. If you take
one very large, reclusive, and eccentric man who lives to eat, add one
young woman fresh out of culinary school who lives to cook, and then
stir in a love of musical comedy and fresh-brewed exotic tea, with just
a hint of magic, will the result be a soufflé—or a charred, inedible mess?

The Lucidity Project by Abbey Campbell Cook. $16.95, 978-1-63152-032-
7. After suffering from depression all her life, twenty-five-year-old Max
Dorigan joins a mysterious research project on a Caribbean island,
where she's introduced to the magical and healing world of lucid
dreaming.

The Tolling of Mercedes Bell by Jennifer Dwight. $18.95, 978-1-63152-070-
9. When she meets a magnetic lawyer at her work, recently widowed
Mercedes Bell unwittingly drinks a noxious cocktail of grief, legal
intrigue, desire, and deception—but when she realizes that her life and
her daughter's safety hang in the balance, she is jolted into action.

Vote for Remi by Leanna Lehman. $16.95, 978-1-63152-978-8. History is
changed forever when an ambitious classroom of high school seniors
pull the ultimate prank on their favorite teacher—and end up getting her
in the running to become president of the United States.

Wishful Thinking by Kamy Wicoff. $16.95, 978-1-63152-976-4. A
divorced mother of two gets an app on her phone that lets her be in
more than one place at the same time, and quickly goes from zero to
hero in her personal and professional life—but at what cost?